PROOF OF INNOCENCE

LENORA WORTH

HARLEQUIN® LOVE INSPIRED® SUSPENSE

Special thanks and acknowledgment are given to Lenora Worth
for their participation in the Capitol K-9 Unit series.

Recycling programs
for this product may
not exist in your area.

 LOVE INSPIRED BOOKS

ISBN-13: 978-0-373-44684-1

Proof of Innocence

Copyright © 2015 by Harlequin Books S.A.

www.Harlequin.com

Printed in U.S.A.

Before destruction the heart of a man is haughty,
And before honor is humility.
—Proverbs 18:12

To my fellow authors in this series: Shirlee McCoy,
Terri Reed, Lynette Eason, Margaret Daley and Valerie Hansen.
I love and appreciate all of you!

ONE

An urgent heartbeat pounded through Erin Eagleton's temples each time her sneakered feet hit the dry, packed earth. She stumbled, grabbed at a leafy sapling and checked behind her again. The tree's slender limbs hit at her face and neck when she let go, leaving welts across her cheekbones, but she kept running. The sun slid in a shimmering-gold descent beyond the trees to the west as dusk settled like a vivid red-orange blanket over the sticky, hot Virginia hillside. Soon it would be full dark and she would have to find a safe place to hide.

Winded and damp with a cold sweat that made her shiver as it snaked down her backbone, Erin tried to catch her breath. Did she dare stop and try to find another path?

The sound of approaching footsteps behind her caused Erin to stare through her nonprescription black-framed glasses into the growing darkness. Making a split-second decision, she took off to the right and headed deeper into the woods. She had to keep running until she came to a highway or a hideaway. But she was so tired. Would she ever be free?

Dear Lord, I'm so lost. I don't know where to turn.

Memories of Chase Zachary moved through her head, causing tears to prick at her eyes. Her first love. Her high school sweetheart who now worked as a K-9 officer with an elite Washington, DC, team. A team that was investigating her.

From what she'd read on the internet and in the local papers, Chase had been one of the first officers on the scene that horrible night.

She'd thought about calling him a hundred times over these past few months, but Erin wasn't sure she could trust even Chase. The last time they'd seen each other, on the very evening this nightmare had taken place, he hadn't been very friendly. And why should he be kind toward her? He probably hated her for breaking his heart when they were so young.

But then just about everybody else along the Beltway and possibly even in the entire metro area surrounding DC hated her right now. Erin had been on the run for months. She knew running made her look guilty, but she'd had no other choice since she'd witnessed the murder of Michael Jeffries, and she'd almost been killed herself. The authorities thought she was the killer and until she could prove otherwise, Erin had to stay hidden.

The media had already condemned her with a relentless assault that had her face plastered all over television news reports and newspaper headlines. Whole hours of cable news had been dedicated to dissecting her life. How could anyone stand up to such scrutiny?

The reports had at first painted her as an allegedly scorned ex-girlfriend who'd possibly murdered prominent Washington lawyer Michael Jeffries because he'd broken up with her. None of which was true. Michael had been too caught up in his crusade against corruption to even have time to break up with her, and besides, their relationship was mostly for "show," to please their political families. Tired of the ruse, *she'd* actually gone to dinner with Michael on that cold night to break things off with *him*. But Michael had been too upset about another situation in his life for her to tell him it was over between them, publicly and privately. He'd found out he might have a young relative living in a foster home and he'd insisted he had to get home and do some more digging for the truth.

Erin still remembered Michael's frantic attempts to explain the situation. "I can't tell you everything, Erin. I don't want to accuse anyone of wrongdoing, but I *will* find out the truth. I think I can prove I'm right. I need more time. And I'm going to talk to my father and make him tell me the truth."

They'd parted ways, and Erin had decided to go for a walk.

Later, concerned about his state of mind, she'd searched for Michael and found him at his father's estate outside the city.

At least the news reports had one thing right about that night. Michael had been murdered.

And she knew who'd killed him because she'd witnessed the whole horrible scene. But no one would believe her if she told the truth—that Congressman Harland Jeffries had killed his own son, had worked to pin the murder on Erin and had tried to have her killed, too.

Now Erin Eagleton was a wanted woman.

And if she couldn't get away from the man chasing her so she could prove her innocence, she'd soon be going to jail.

Or—she'd soon be dead.

* * *

Chase Zachary held the delicate cashmere scarf to his nose, the lingering scent of the expensive floral perfume making him remember the touch of her lips on his. Chase remembered way too many things about the girl he'd loved and lost years ago in high school. But right now he'd give anything to find Erin once again.

Help me, Lord. Help me to find her before it's too late.

She was out here in these woods, lost and afraid. Chase had been searching for her for close to five months, while on duty and often on his own time, too. He'd never believed Erin capable of murdering Congressman Jeffries's son Michael and shooting the congressman, so he'd been trying to find enough evidence to disprove the original theory that had her as the scorned girlfriend who'd been at the scene of the crime. So many things about this case didn't add up, but at least now they had a witness who said the congressman *had* shot his son.

That witness, an aide named Leon Ridge, was now in custody. After being caught a few days ago after planting a bomb, he'd finally caved and explained that the congressman had accidentally shot Michael and then, in an effort to cover it up, he'd had Leon shoot him so he could insist that some unseen assailant had attacked both of them. And the congressman had hinted that Erin might be involved. Crazy, but Leon had done a good job following orders. The congressman's injuries had been severe enough to make it look real, but Leon Ridge swore his version was the truth.

"And what about Erin Eagleton?" Chase had asked the bouncer of an aide. Rumor around the city was that

Leon's only qualification involved handling delicate matters for the congressman.

"I don't know anything about her," Leon had retorted. Then he'd started fidgeting.

"You mean you haven't heard all the news reports alleging she was the shooter? She's missing, in case you didn't know."

"I don't watch the news."

"Right. But you probably know that Congressman Jeffries is wanted on corruption charges. He's missing. Could have left the country."

Shock had turned Leon's skin a sickly pale.

The captain had stood up. "Let us know when you're ready to tell us what really happened that night, Ridge. Think about it long and hard because until we find Erin Eagleton and the congressman, you're our main suspect."

"Hey, I told you the truth. The congressman accidentally shot his son."

"And you were forced to shoot him at his request to make it look like an unknown assailant did it," Chase had reminded him. "That's a tall tale, for sure." Then he'd asked Leon Ridge the one question burning through him. "Was Erin at the congressman's estate that night?"

"Like I said," Ridge had insisted in a quick rush of breath, "I don't know anything about Erin Eagleton."

Ridge still maintained he was telling the truth, but Chase didn't believe him. More like, he was covering his own hide until Erin turned up. Ridge had clammed up even more when two fancy lawyers had visited him.

Now Erin was still out there on the run, afraid for her life. Chase needed to find her to tell her that they had new information that might clear her name.

And he wanted to tell her that it had all started with a two-year-old boy.

A maid named Rosa Gomez who worked for the congressman had been found dead the day before Michael Jeffries was shot. The congressman was wounded the night Michael died and at first claimed he hadn't seen the shooter. Erin's starfish necklace was found at the scene of the shooting—Chase had verified that since he'd seen her earlier on the night of the shooting. After that, everything pointed to Erin as a witness or person of interest, but no one had been able to find her.

Then a kid named Tommy Benson from the All Our Kids foster home not far from the congressman's estate confessed that he'd sneaked out that night and witnessed the congressman holding a gun. But the kid also said Michael was still alive when he was there. Tommy hadn't seen Erin there. He didn't even recognize her in a picture. Chase couldn't imagine Erin arriving after that and committing such a cold-blooded crime. No way.

But things were unraveling for the pompous congressman. The dead maid had left behind a little boy who carried the same scallop-shaped light brown birthmark as the congressman and his son Michael. Strong evidence that the rumors about the boy being Harland Jeffries's son could be true. And maybe…it was one of the reasons Michael had been murdered. Congressman Jeffries stood to lose everything if he'd been having an affair with his maid and had a secret child whom he'd let languish in foster care.

But would that alone force him to kill his adult son?

The team had finally found evidence of corruption by the congressman…in his own meticulous records. They'd also had a break when they'd arrested several of his top aides, but no one wanted to talk. They'd planned to bring in Congressman Harland Jeffries on corruption charges and to question him about the murdered maid since the evidence was mounting on that one, too. But the congressman had fled. No one could locate him and Leon Ridge talked only about his version of what had happened the night Michael had died.

But Ridge had admitted to planting a bomb to kill K-9 team member Isaac Black and DC General Hospital nurse Daniella Dunne, trying to make it look as if Daniella's mobster father, Terence Fagan, had done the job. Congressman Jeffries knew the nurse had seen his birthmark, the same birthmark that Michael and little Juan Gomez had on their shoulder. More evidence that Juan was a Jeffries.

That admission at least showed Leon Ridge as a henchman for the congressman and proved that the congressman wanted the Capitol K-9 team to stop this investigation.

Ridge was a witness to whatever really happened the night Michael was murdered, but he refused to even discuss Erin's involvement.

Someone had put a muzzle on Ridge. Why?

Was the congressman trying to get to Erin before she could finally tell the truth about what happened at his estate that night?

"I know you didn't do this," Chase said, his gaze scanning the countryside. Fiona Fargo, who worked as a technician for the team, had been helping to track any chatter regarding Congressman Jeffries or Erin Eagleton, and had seen some interesting search efforts in the internet cafés in and around this area. When she'd found a Wi-Fi hot spot at a local hotel, she'd let the team know some of the searches might be coming from Erin. And she'd found evidence that Erin was picking up work there as a waitress. That explained how she had cash to carry her through.

Chase hoped he could find Erin soon, and he wished he could have helped her the night of the murder, or at least stopped her from going to the Jeffries estate. But they'd bumped into each other near the Washington Monument and the tension between them had somehow overshadowed any clear thinking.

She hadn't even realized Chase was jogging along the path until he stopped and called her name. "Erin?"

Erin had whirled, her honey-blond curls collapsing in a silky waterfall around her face and shoulders. She wore a patterned scarf bundled loosely around her shoulders and a short wool jacket over jeans and high-heeled boots. A gold necklace sparkled against her skin and the blue pattern in the cream-colored scarf matched her deep blue eyes.

"Hey, Chase." Her gaze moved over his fleece hoodie and back to his face, surprise masking her obvious discomfort. "Still staying in shape, huh?"

He jogged in place, and then relaxed. "Yep. Part of the job."

She walked closer, her arms wrapped against her midsection to ward off the winter chill. He could see she'd been crying.

"Are you okay?"

Lowering her head, she looked down at her boots. "I'm fine. Just working through some things." She stared off into the lights twinkling all around the city. "I wonder if it'll snow tonight."

Her tone suggested she didn't want to talk about anything but the weather.

Chase had never known when to give up, however. "Erin, are you sure you're all right? You shouldn't be out here alone."

"I told you, I'm fine."

He tried one more time. Seeing her made his life hard, but he cherished their brief encounters all the same. "Anything I can do?"

She shook her head and wiped at her eyes. "No, nothing. I have to go." She pivoted, her eyes holding his. "It was…good to see you again, Chase."

Chase reached out to her, his fingers brushing against her scarf. "Erin, you know I'd do anything for you, no matter what."

"I don't need your help," she replied, ripping away from his touch. "Not anymore."

That comment brought out a pent-up bitterness in Chase. "You mean, because you don't need me in your life now, right? I saw you with Michael Jeffries at that recent White House dinner. I guess your father is still calling the shots."

"I have my own life now, Chase. No one tells me what to do."

"Okay," he said, hating himself for caring. "Or maybe you still don't have the courage to stand up to your daddy."

The hurt in her eyes as she turned away made Chase want to take back that accusation. But it was too late for that. Too late for a lot of things.

"Erin?"

"I have to go," she'd said, her expression as chilly as

the night wind blustering through the bare branches of the nearby cherry trees.

She'd taken off so fast her scarf fell away from her jacket. The soft material fluttered toward the ground like a dying butterfly, but Chase caught it up in his hands.

Chase had held it and called out to her. "Erin?"

But she'd already slipped out of sight.

Chase had been one of the last people to see her the day of the murder, and he'd beaten himself up over that tense conversation. What had she been crying about that night? Why hadn't she let him help her?

A few hours later, he'd seen her broken starfish necklace in an evidence bag and Chase had become obsessed with finding Erin. It might be too late for them, but he wouldn't let time run out on saving her.

This latest lead from Fiona and the research team had brought him to a rural area of Virginia about forty miles southwest of DC. Months ago, someone matching Erin's description had been seen by a couple, Edward and Mavis Appleton. The elderly Virginia husband and wife had helped Erin in the days after the murder, but they'd been attacked by some thugs also looking for Erin. Since then, no one had come forward with any concrete sightings, but the team had proof that she'd been using internet cafés and remote libraries to do some online research, all of it pointing toward a strong corruption case against the supposedly upstanding Congressman Jeffries. Smart. She'd tried to bring down Jeffries on her own.

Since the man was now wanted on said corruption charges, Erin had obviously been onto the truth. Because the congressman had fled and was now missing,

Chase wanted to find Erin before one of the congressman's henchmen did.

The big dog at his feet whimpered and danced around, dark eyes staring up at Chase with anxious clarity. Valor was ready to get on with things, too.

"Yeah, boy, I know," Chase said to his K-9 partner. Trained in search and rescue, Valor knew only that he was needed to find someone. But how could Chase explain to his faithful companion that they'd gone off the grid—way off the grid?

Leaning down, Chase allowed the fawn-colored Belgian Malinois to sniff the now-familiar cream-and-blue patterned cashmere scarf.

"We need to find her, Valor," he said, praying that after so many months of uncertainty regarding Erin Eagleton's whereabouts, one of his leads would finally pay off.

Valor sniffed the delicate material, then started trembling. The big dog was ready to go. Chase held tight to the leash and made sure Valor's protective vest was secure. Then he gave the command to "Find."

Valor took off into the Virginia woods located along a jogging trail near a narrow stream. Chase held tight and ran along with the animal. Had they hit on something so soon?

Was Erin somewhere nearby?

TWO

She was running in circles. Every tree hulked like a giant monster waiting to grab her. Every snap of a branch caused her to whirl in a dizzy spin of fear and slap at some unseen assailant. Earlier, unable to sleep, she'd heard someone outside her room—and she'd seen a man dressed in dark clothing and carrying a gun. Erin hadn't stayed around to see if he'd come to call on her. She was used to mysterious assailants trying to kill her. Going out the back and over the balcony, she'd taken the first path into the dense woods, thinking she could circle back and hide somewhere in the small town and then board a bus out. Somehow.

Now it was dark and she was soaked with sweat and the bugs were trying to finish her off. The short dark auburn wig she wore seemed to be shrinking on her head. It pressed into her skull like a wet mesh helmet and had her whole head itching with a fire that burned all the way down her backbone. The few possessions she managed to carry around bounced together in the deep pocket of the old jeans she'd been wearing for days now. She had a little cash left and she had her research notebook. She sure didn't want to lose that since it had all her memories and all of her questions and, maybe, a few answers. Erin had to get somewhere safe before morning. Another hotel with a front and back entry, so she wouldn't be cornered, more attempts to search online for information and clues, news articles and tips.

This was her life now, a never-ending nightmare of always looking over her shoulder with an ingrained fear that might not ever leave her. She was pretty sure she'd finally outrun her pursuer, so she planned to hike out of the woods.

Searching for any sign of the lights toward the town, she shifted in the gray moonlight and slid behind a big tree. What was that sound? Was someone running toward her again?

Footsteps echoed out over the woods and the swish of bushes being shoved aside followed. Someone was still after her.

Holding her breath, Erin closed her eyes and prayed for guidance. She would survive this. She'd heard the news reports regarding the vast array of corruption charges being brought up against Congressman Jeffries. Now he'd been indicted for some of his crimes. But surprise—he'd fled like the coward he was. At least she wouldn't have to be the one to prove he was corrupt. But she still had to prove she hadn't killed Michael. She knew the truth and she intended to tell that truth once she…once she what?

Turned herself in and tried to reason with the police?

Or maybe gave a long statement over the airwaves and screamed to the world that she was on the right side of the law?

Or maybe she could call her powerful father and hope that the scandal of having a fugitive daughter hadn't ruined his position in the Senate or severed his strong ties with the Washington elite. But she'd been careful about not having contact with her father so she couldn't start now. He'd have to report hearing from her. Knowing that being involved in such a scandal could indeed ruin her father's career right along with any thoughts she had of her life going back to normal, Erin didn't know where to turn next.

She dropped her head and stood there, defeated and exhausted. When she heard pounding footsteps coming toward her, she knew she had no choice. She had to run as fast as she could.

But a thought occurred to her. In the cover of darkness, she could at least try to stop the gunman in his tracks before she took off. She'd trip him up and try to hit him over the head, maybe use some of the self-defense maneuvers her father had his security team teach her. That had worked when the congressman's aide Leon Ridge had tried to kill her the night of the murder. Maybe she could find the strength to fight off this latest assailant.

Erin crouched behind a huge live oak's aged trunk, a broken limb her only means of protection. She waited, holding her breath, her mind whirling with the vision of her hitting her stalker over the head, tripping him with one foot while she hit at him with all her might. Then she'd run. As fast as she could.

But when she turned to put her foot out, a dog's woof caused her to stumble. Right into two waiting hands.

Erin started fighting, kicking and screaming as she tried to gain a foothold.

The dog started barking but stood back in a frenzied dance.

And the man holding her did something that surprised her and caused her whole world to tilt.

He shouted "Heel" at the big dog, and then he called her by her name. "Erin? Erin? It's me. It's Chase."

Erin stopped fighting, her fists relaxing against his solid chest, her gaze halting on the face she remembered so well. Her voice cracked and she blinked to clear her head. "Chase?"

"It's okay," he said on a whisper. "You're safe now, understand? You're with me now and I won't let anything happen to you."

"Chase." She said his name on the wings of a prayer and thanked God for sending her a hero. *Chase Zachary.* A hero who had once been the love of her life, her high school sweetheart.

A man who'd also been after her for over five months.

Should she try to run from him, too?

She hadn't asked for this and she wasn't prepared for what seeing Chase now could mean, but for a few brief seconds, she was so very glad to see him again. "Chase? Is it really you?"

"Yes." His fingers gentled on her skin. "Relax, okay?"

Then he pulled her into his arms and held her close while she cried. Somewhere in the back of her frayed mind, she heard the big dog woof again. But this time the sound only reinforced how relieved she felt. Relieved and safe—unless he planned to take her into custody.

"Where are you taking me?"

Erin couldn't quite wrap her brain around Chase finding her in these lonely, isolated woods. But when she glanced ahead at the dog leading them through the overgrown bramble and tangled vines, she understood. He'd had a little help from a friend. She could try to run again, but the dog would track her down. A weight of fatigue pulled at her like a heavy, stifling blanket. The enormity of Chase finding her caught up with her until panic set in. She had to run. These people would kill her and Chase, too.

Did she really want to go back out there alone? No. So she asked again, "Chase, where are we going?"

"Away from this place," he said, his words just above a growl.

Earlier when she'd explained someone had been after her, Chase had quickly checked the woods before moving on, and then he'd made sure he and the dog guarded her at all times. They'd zigzagged back and forth, the dog stopping here and there to sniff the wind and the ground, but never alerting. Chase hadn't made any small talk. He was intent on doing his job—which she figured now meant keeping her alive until he could get her under lock and key. Maybe the gunman who'd stalked her was gone. But she knew others would keep coming.

She thanked God the dog had led Chase to her at a time when she'd been out of options. But that joy was short-lived. "You tracked me."

He nodded, his hand still on her arm. But then he stopped and tugged something out from under his shirt and shoved it at her. "I believe this belongs to you."

Erin took the soft white-tinged bundle, but it was hard to see what it was in the dark. The material glistened in the moonlight and she let out a gasp. "My elephant scarf. How did you—"

"You dropped it the last time we talked."

Erin swallowed back the emotional agony that

scraped across her frazzled nerve endings. Their chance meeting so many months ago had stayed with her all this time. They'd had a brief argument that night just hours before Michael had died. Chase had made a sarcastic remark about seeing her at a White House dinner with Michael. He'd accused her of never being able to stand up to her formidable daddy. And he had been right. She was such a coward, she'd been afraid to tell anyone what had happened later that same night—the night she'd watched the congressman shoot Michael.

She'd been afraid to contact her father, afraid the congressman would make good on his threats to kill her father or ruin his career. And she'd been afraid to reach out to the one man who could have possibly helped her. The man now guiding her out of the dark woods.

And yet Chase had kept her scarf. "You've had this all this time?"

"Yep. I asked your father if I could hold on to it—to help track you."

Chase had gone to her father? Of course they'd have to cooperate with each other regarding her whereabouts. She wondered how many times the authorities had questioned the senator. She could never be sure of her father's true motives, but she loved him dearly and since her mother had died, Erin had tried to be the good daughter everyone expected her to be. She wanted to believe the senator would tell the truth no matter what. He'd taught her that much at least. Erin had managed to stay away from her father while on the run, so he wouldn't be forced to lie on her behalf. But she missed him so much.

"Is he okay?" she asked, tears hot in her eyes. She'd heard her father had been injured in an attack a few weeks ago, and she'd managed to sneak into a DC hospital to check on him but only long enough to make sure he wasn't seriously hurt. He never knew she was there. But she wasn't ready to admit that to Chase.

"Your father is fine," he answered. "He's concerned about you, of course."

Chase obviously didn't want to discuss the man who'd come between them when they were so young and full of idealistic love. But then, Chase wasn't one to discuss his feelings with anybody.

"I'm sure he's concerned," she replied, wishing she could explain everything to Chase right now. "And the Eagleton Foundation? Any word on that?"

"Kind of in a holding pattern from what we've heard. We questioned everyone who works for the foundation. No one knew anything about your whereabouts." He gave her a quick glance. "They're all concerned about you."

She'd probably be voted out as CEO of the Eagleton Foundation. If that hadn't already happened.

"I couldn't contact anyone. It would have put them in danger, too."

He didn't respond to that, but he shot her a cautious glance and guided her over a tree root.

Holding on to the scarf like a lifeline, Erin loved the softness it brought back into her life. Knowing Chase had carried her scarf all these months gave her renewed hope. But the memories the exquisite piece of her past life brought out made her want to weep. She was no longer that girl and she was no longer a part of Washington's elite society either. The nation's capital was a very unforgiving place.

But she had her memories, good and bad. "My dad

gave me this scarf for my birthday a few years ago. You know how I love animals."

Chase glanced over at her. "Yep. I remember you going on a safari…one summer."

The summer after they'd broken up.

Erin wrapped the delicate cream material stamped with blue elephants around her neck. "Chase, are you taking me back to DC?"

"No."

Thinking he'd never been a man of words, she tried again. "Where are we going?"

"Where were you before?"

And so like him to answer a question with a question.

"In a hotel up on the highway." They wound around a curve in the path. "I've tried to stay in cheap hotels to save cash. I've worked odd jobs to keep me going."

Which he had to have known. He'd found her, hadn't he? Was he testing her for the truth?

If so, he didn't let on. "Then we won't be going back to any of those places. They'll be looking for you at every cheap motel in the area."

They finally emerged from the woods and she saw a white SUV with official trim work and the words *Capitol K-9 Unit* stamped in dark letters on its sides. In bright red underneath, it stated *Caution. Police Dog.* Chase and the dog he'd called Valor stopped, both of them shielding her while the man did a visual of the area and the dog lifted his nose for any air scents.

"He's beautiful," she said after Chase used his key fob to open the high-tech vehicle. He helped her into the passenger's seat, where what looked like an assault rifle was mounted inside the console between the seats. Valor jumped into a clean metal compartment right behind the two front seats, his doleful dark eyes washing over Erin with a certain curiosity that belied his training.

She automatically held her knuckles to his brown nose and allowed him to get to know her. "Hey there, Valor. Thank you so much for finding me."

Valor whimpered a reply and did a little dance to show he understood. Chase patted the dog's head and made sure he had some water. Then he closed the side door and got into the SUV.

"He's a hard worker," he said while he buckled up and checked the area again. Once he appeared satisfied that no one was lurking in the woods, he let out a sigh. "Erin, are you okay? Really?"

Did he actually care how she felt? "I am now."

He nodded and she could almost feel his gaze hot on her skin. She'd thought about his green eyes a lot when she'd been trudging through lush hills full of birch and hickory trees and old mushrooming oaks. Her heart lifted, but a solid dread brought it back down to earth. Would Chase understand her predicament?

He watched the shadows around the vehicle and then glanced over at her. "Then tell me what's going on."

She was so glad to be able to talk to someone she needed to trust that she pulled off the offending wig and tugged at the fake eyeglasses. Her now chin-length hair tumbled out in damp dark tufts of mixed brown and blond highlights. "Someone was chasing me. Again."

"We've established that," he said, his gaze moving over her hair. "I need to know the whole story, starting with the night you went missing."

Erin tried to detangle her curls. "You might not believe the whole story."

"Try me."

She wanted to tell him everything so he could help her piece it all together. "Can we find someplace else to discuss this? I've been hiding out so long and I hate these woods." She glanced out the window. "I have a mortal fear that someone is always watching me."

He cranked the big SUV. "Okay, but… I'm about to make a call to Captain McCord and… I need to know one thing first and what I tell him will depend entirely on your answer to my question."

"What do you need to know, Chase?" she asked, already understanding. Already seeing reluctance in his doubtful, hopeful gaze.

He held on to the steering wheel with both hands, but his gaze held hers. "Did you murder Michael Jeffries?"

Erin understood he had to ask, but her heart hurt at hearing that question coming from his lips. "No," she said. "No, Chase. I didn't murder Michael. But I know who did."

Then she went on before he could say anything. "And before you make that call, I need to know if I can trust *you*." She slanted her head and stared him down. "Do you believe me?"

"Yes," he said without hesitation. "I told you—you're safe now."

"Okay," she said, her shoulders feeling as if a great weight had been shoved off them. "Make the call."

He heaved a breath then took out his cell and asked to speak to Captain Gavin McCord. Erin listened and held her breath while Chase gave the captain his location.

His next words startled her. "I have Erin Eagleton with me and I hope to be able to…bring her in soon." Chase listened and then replied, "Yes, sir. I understand.

It's late and she's exhausted. I plan on stopping for the night to throw anyone off our trail."

Erin lifted her chin and pivoted on the seat. Had he tricked her? Would he turn her over to the DC authorities and just walk away?

She'd get out of this car and take off again if he planned to do that.

But when Chase ended the call, he turned to her. "Okay, I bought us some time, but Captain McCord is probably calling General Margaret Meyer right now to read her in on this. Meantime, I'm going to find us a safe place to stay tonight so we can talk. Just you and me."

Just you and me.

His stoic, matter-of-fact words held a hint of intimacy that only reminded her of their time together.

As if to cover that, he said, "I need to hear the whole story from you before things get chaotic."

Erin put a hand on his arm. "Thank you."

He didn't say anything, but she saw the way he glanced down at her finger curled against his arm. The heat between them radiated like a warm wind that rivaled the humid summer night. She moved her hand away and he put the vehicle in Reverse and took the bumpy dirt path to the main road. Soon they were speeding away into the night.

Since she didn't have to watch over her shoulder at every turn, Erin relaxed for the first time in a long while. Chase was here. But so many questions remained between them. Maybe Chase would help her sort out all of this before Congressman Jeffries found her and silenced her forever.

"Rest," he said. "We'll figure this out, I promise."

· Erin leaned her head against the car door, his words echoing in her head as she drifted into the first peaceful sleep she'd had in months.

THREE

Chase put his hand on Erin's shoulder. She'd fallen asleep almost immediately after they'd left the deserted park about twenty miles back. He'd driven in circles for at least an hour and he'd watched the road for anyone who might be following them. Now he was on a remote back road where a sign boasted a bed-and-breakfast that promised privacy.

He'd have to do a quick sweep with Valor after they checked in, but maybe this place would be safe for the night at least.

"Erin?"

She jumped and grabbed at his hand then started hitting and slapping him, a scream tearing through her throat.

"Erin, it's me. Chase!"

She gulped in deep breaths, her eyes wide with fear and then awareness. Her whole body relaxing, she asked, "Where...where are we?"

"An old inn. Way off the beaten path." He had to take her inside and find her some food and a good soft bed so she could get some sleep. Handing her a generic navy-colored ball cap he kept in the SUV, he said, "Put your hair up underneath this and put those glasses back on."

"I have the wig," she said on a groggy note.

Chase did a visual and saw nothing but dark woods and the winding road up to the inn. "But someone's seen you in that wig," he retorted. "Put on the cap until I can get you in a room."

"Okay."

Her meek tone tore through Chase. Erin wasn't one to be meek or subdued. She was honest and frank and smart. Never afraid and never this quiet. She'd gone on the run for a reason and Chase believed that reason consisted of staying alive so she could prove her innocence. But it also showed him that right now, she didn't trust anyone. Especially not him.

Trying to ignore the disturbing feelings being near her seemed to be unleashing, he helped her with her now-mismatched hair. She'd obviously dyed it a couple of times. And she'd cut it. Still shorter than he remembered, it hit in soft waves against her chin. He remembered the softness of her hair, remembered pulling the light caramel-colored strands through his fingers so he could tug her close. Now he had to keep a safe distance. And keep her safe.

He had to stop reliving the past and start focusing on keeping her alive. That was his duty.

Your duty was to find her and bring her in for questioning.

He planned to question Erin. A lot. He'd report in again after he'd heard her side of things.

But he wasn't letting her out of his sight until he knew the truth. He figured there was much more to this story and he didn't know whom he could trust right now.

So Chase did what he'd always done when he had doubts.

He went with his instincts. And his instincts told him that this woman would never hurt another human being. Much less kill one. Now he just had to match her story with what Leon Ridge had told them. Maybe soon, they'd all know the truth.

The Moonlight Inn lived up to its name. The big Victorian house glistened with an eerie grayish-white wash from the light of a crescent moon. Surrounded by towering old live oaks, it looked at once both welcoming and sinister.

Erin loved the quaint old white clapboard exterior with the wraparound porch, but she wasn't so sure about the isolation of the place. Still, being away from the main road allowed Chase and her some time to get all the facts straight. If she could keep her eyes open long enough to talk to him. It took all she had to put one foot in front of the other.

"You look plum wore out," the cheerful lady behind the front desk said, her concerned brown eyes washing over Erin's soiled T-shirt and jeans with a keen interest. "Did you two go on a long hike today?"

"Yes," Chase answered with a smile. He glanced down at Valor. "And we chased this fellow around a lot. We're ready to settle in for the night."

The woman's gaze moved from Erin to the dog at their feet. "What a beautiful animal."

"Thank you," Chase said. He'd already removed Valor's working vest so no one would ask too many questions. "He's tired, too. He loves to…search the countryside."

"Chasing squirrels, huh, boy?" The lady chuckled, her white hair as stiff as the fake pink flowers clustered in a pretty red vase next to the antique cash register.

The woman glanced at Erin, causing Erin to realize that she hadn't spoken.

"Yes, always chasing something," she said, her tone forced. Chase hadn't clarified anything with the desk clerk. Erin wondered how he'd handle the room situation.

"If it's available, we'd like the deluxe suite with the sitting room," he said, pointing to some pictures underneath the glass on the counter.

The old lady nodded. "Our best suite. Roomy and private."

Chase didn't respond. He simply paid the bill and kept smiling. Erin took in her surroundings, a habit she'd developed after being forced to watch her back. The inn was clean and uncluttered with the front entrance and lobby here and a long hallway to the back of the house. If she had to run…

"All set," the woman said, handing Chase a receipt. "I hope you have a good stay."

Chase glanced toward Erin, his green eyes going soft. "Thanks. I hope so, too."

Erin managed a smile to hide the way her throat tightened and went dry at that glance. Now that they were inside, the glow from the lamplight clearly showed her all the features of his face for the first time.

He'd aged into someone she recognized and yet didn't really know. His dark blond hair was cut in a crisp military style that stood in curling spikes across his forehead, and he had a few laugh lines, or maybe worry lines, around his eyes. He was buff and tan and healthy. Her heart, which had shriveled up in a corner to die when she'd lost all hope, seemed to unfold like a blossoming rose. She didn't want to depend on this man. She could turn and bolt out the door, but she was so weary. She felt safe just being near him.

Chase looked as good as she remembered and then some.

While she was dirty and tired and mousy. And then some. A far cry from her sorority days and the whirlwind social life of the nation's capital.

But she was relieved. She couldn't help the relief that pushed through her numb system like a cooling wind to prove she was still alive. This kind of comfort could come only from knowing someone she'd once loved had found her when she thought she'd be lost forever. Erin glanced at a still life on the wall of a stream flowing down a mountainside. This was how she felt each time she sat in the dark and prayed, the image of Christ front and center in her frazzled mind. Lately, she'd almost given up on that image. But Chase stood here, an answer to a prayer she hadn't even known she'd prayed.

"There you go," the woman with the name tag that said *Janey* told them. "You're all set. Breakfast is from six until nine each day and if you'd like, I can send up a midnight snack to tide you over. Since you're arriving so late and all." She glanced at the go bag Chase had grabbed from the SUV and then she let her gaze sweep over Erin's torn, dirt-stained jeans, old hoodie and ratty T-shirt. "There's a washer/dryer combination in the hallway to my left if you need to wash some clothes."

Chase didn't take her up on that offer. "We'll take the snack. With hot tea and coffee."

"And I'd like some water," Erin added, touched that

he remembered her preference for hot tea. "With lots of ice."

"Okay. I'll get right on that." The woman smiled at Erin. "And you can enjoy a good, long bath, honey."

"That sounds perfect," Erin replied, true joy racing through her heart. It had been a long time since she'd had a bubble bath.

But when they got upstairs, she watched Chase checking all the windows and doors and decided that in spite of the wonderful, old-fashioned claw-footed tub in the adjoining bathroom, she might not get that bath. A quick shower would have to suffice.

Because they didn't have time for the luxuries. Chase was here on a mission to either bring her in as a wanted murder suspect, or to help her prove her innocence.

And tonight was all about her convincing him on which option he should choose.

Chase took Valor for a quick walk, telling the way-too-interested Janey that the big dog needed to have a bathroom break. She nodded and explained where the dog walk was located. That was fine by Chase since it allowed him a chance to patrol the perimeters of the property and check around bushes and shrubs. Satisfied that the place was secure for now, he glanced up at the window where the deluxe suite was located. The room where Erin sat right now, jotting down notes she wanted to present to him when he got back. A small balcony was centered near two French doors, but it should be safe since it would be difficult for anyone to climb up the side of the house to get in. Difficult, but with a big oak tree nearby, it could be done if a person was determined. He and Valor would keep watch all night.

When they turned back toward the front door, Chase heard a twig snap down past the slope in the yard. Valor's ears went up while Chase's system buzzed with a new awareness.

He could release Valor to search, but this could be a trap, a means of distraction to draw them away from the house.

Not wanting to take any chances, he kept an eye on the front entrance and hurried Valor along so they could get back. He'd already had a quick shower, but a new sheen of perspiration worked its way down his spine, and not from the snap of a twig. Erin Eagleton had always made him sweat.

It had been obvious from their first glance several years ago that Erin was way out of his league. She'd been the popular socialite cheerleader at the small, private high school they'd both attended. And Chase had been the poor kid who'd been given a football scholarship to the school where all the politicians' children had first dibs on everything. She'd lived in one of the gated estates that dotted the countryside surrounding Washington and he'd lived in a standard farmhouse that his hardworking family had hung on to for nearly a century.

First class meets middle class and love at first sight for him. Maybe even for her. They'd both fallen hard, and then they'd been torn apart way too soon.

But that was all over now. Erin had been dating Michael Jeffries for years. No way she could have killed him.

It had been common knowledge that Erin and Michael were considered a power couple along the Beltway. She was the beautiful daughter of a popular senator and Michael was the son of Congressman Harland Jeffries. She and Michael were often seen together all over Washington, attending high-level parties and dinners. The kind of parties that a rookie K-9 officer who was former Secret Service usually patrolled rather than attended.

Reminding himself that he was part of an elite unit of officers, soldiers and special agents who had been handpicked by the president's special in-house security chief, Margaret Meyer, Chase hoped he could earn his merit by bringing Erin back alive so they could get to the truth.

She was here and safe for the time being. He hurried back upstairs, remembering how she'd looked in a huge white terry cloth robe she'd found in the closet, thrown over a pair of black running shorts and a T-shirt he'd dug from his go-bag. At least the extra clothes had been clean. Baggy and cute on her, but clean.

And she looked…beautiful.

Tired, worried, fragile and beautiful.

It had taken a lot of willpower for him not to rush across the room and hold on to her forever. They might not have forever if he couldn't clear her name. They might not have a forever even after he cleared her name. Erin would want to go back to her posh life and leave him to get on with his simple life.

Which now only reminded Chase that he didn't have time to go down memory lane and he sure didn't have time for daydreams of how Erin looked all fresh faced and blushing.

Waving good-night to Janey—did the woman ever go to sleep?—he took the stairs two at a time and rapped on the locked door twice. "It's Chase."

Erin opened the door with a cup of tea in her hand.

Someone from the staff had brought up food earlier. He'd checked the waiter and the food and waited for her to come out of the bathroom so they could eat. But his appetite had disappeared at the sight of her. Using the excuse of walking the dog, he'd bolted out of the suite with a terse order for her to lock all the doors and stay put.

Now he was hungry. For food. For her story. For just being with her again. "Mind if I eat while we talk?"

"No," she said, motioning to the pushcart full of tiny crustless sandwiches along with fruit and cheese and two giant chocolate chip cookies. "Your coffee is in that little pot." She pointed to a silver carafe.

Chase settled Valor with a treat and then came to sit on a cushiony blue love seat across from her cream-colored leather chair. After downing two of the ham-and-cheese sandwiches, he poured some coffee and rubbed a hand over his hair. "Everything looked okay outside. We should be safe for the night."

She nodded. "I can't seem to stay awake."

"That's the letdown," he explained. "You've been living on adrenaline for months now."

"Oh, and here I thought I was just tired." She bit into a slice of rich cheddar cheese and grabbed a couple of plump grapes.

"You *are* tired, but… Erin, before things get crazy tomorrow, I need to hear the whole story and then I'll tell you what I know."

He didn't want to give her any details that might color her own perception or blur her story. They could compare notes after he got her statement down.

She put down her tea and pushed away the plate of food. "Okay." Then she took a deep breath and tugged the big robe around her. After picking up her crumbled notebook, she opened it as if she were about to read a book. Then she slapped it shut and lifted her gaze to meet his.

"I had planned to break things off with Michael," she began. "Our fathers pushed us together in our last year of college, but honestly, we never got past being friends. We had fun together and I guess you could say we looked good together, according to the tabloids anyway, but it was mostly for show."

Chase took that in as he remembered Erin in flowing formal gowns and on the arm of the man known as "The Capitol Crusader." Michael Jeffries had been a bit cocky and smug, but the man at least had a good heart since he fought for less fortunate people. He sure didn't deserve to be shot even if he had made Chase jealous at times. Chase always told himself Erin was better off with someone who had as much money and clout as her father. That's the way the senator saw things anyway.

"So you did see Michael on the night that he died?"

Erin took a sip of tea and then continued. "Yes, I did. That morning he called me and asked if we could go to dinner and…well, he was so upset when he picked me up I didn't have the heart to break up with him."

Chase jotted notes since this was a new development. "Why was he upset?"

She pushed at her still-damp hair. "He said he'd found out a young relative of his was stuck in foster care and possibly living at the All Our Kids home—you know the one that his father started years ago. Michael was determined to get the child out, but he wouldn't tell me who the kid was or why doing this was so important to him." She shrugged and looked down at her hands. "We parted at around nine or so, but later—not long after I saw you—he didn't answer my calls and I got worried about him."

Chase checked his notes. "You and I spoke around ten that night," he reminded her. "I remember glancing at my watch and wondering why you were out walking so late."

"I needed to think about things," she replied. "I was worried about Michael's frame of mind and I was upset that...I couldn't make it work with him. I went to his condo to check on him and he wasn't there. I figured he'd driven out to his father's estate to possibly discuss getting the congressman's help with this child he was so worried about. He told me he needed to talk to his father, so I headed out there."

Chase held up a hand and decided he could tell her what he knew for a fact. "Let's stop for a minute. We've confirmed that Michael was talking about a two-year-old boy who belonged to his father's housekeeper, Rosa Gomez—"

She shook her head and held her hand toward him. "But then the child couldn't be related to him."

Chase hated to spill things to her in this way, but he had to get all the facts straight and he had to feed them to her one by one. "Erin, the little boy—Juan Gomez—is the son of the congressman. We've pretty much established that he's Michael's half brother."

FOUR

Erin went still, her eyes widening. "I can't believe this. Do you think…Michael went to his father's house to confront him or to at least ask him to take Juan out of foster care?" Then she gasped. "They were in a heated argument when I came around the corner to the patio. What if that's why the congressman shot Michael?"

It was Chase's turn to be shocked. Leon Ridge had told them it was an accident. "Are you saying that's what happened that night?"

She nodded, tears forming in her eyes. "Yes, Chase. I went there to find Michael and…I walked up on them arguing. The congressman said something about Michael ruining everything. He reached for a gun and then they were struggling, pushing and shoving, and the next thing I knew the gun went off and…Michael fell to the ground." She put a hand to her heart. "Then blood went everywhere and…I screamed and ran toward Michael."

Chase saw the terror in her eyes. "And then what happened?"

"I took off my jacket and tried to stop the bleeding. Congressman Jeffries stood there in shock, or so I thought. He tried to explain that it was an accident, but I saw him hold that gun to Michael's stomach and pull the trigger.

"After that, I didn't know what to say, but I kept begging him to call for help. He didn't move and then he turned nasty and pointed the gun at me, telling me if I told anyone what I'd witnessed he'd swear that I shot Michael. When I took out my phone, he grabbed it from me and even threatened to kill my father."

She gulped in a breath. "When I begged him to call 911, he said he'd ruin my father, that he'd frame him and destroy his career. He asked me if I wanted that on my conscience." She put a hand to her mouth and shook her head. "I didn't know what to do."

Chase got up and came to kneel in front of her. "Hey, it's okay. If you're telling the truth and Michael did know about Juan Gomez, we have more than enough information to prove his father had a strong motive for shooting him."

"I am telling the truth," she said, pushing him away. "Why would I lie?"

Chase didn't think she was lying, but he had to keep questioning her. "Why didn't you call your dad or even me? Why did you run, Erin?"

She lifted her head and stared at Chase, her dark blue eyes still moist. "One of the congressman's goons showed up when I was trying to help Michael. Leon Ridge—that creepy aide who was always hanging around. I asked him to help me and that's when the congressman told his aide to rip off the starfish necklace Michael had given me for my birthday and to drop it near Michael's body—and then he demanded that Leon shoot *him* in the shoulder so it would look like I'd done it. But before he let that stupid man shoot him, he told Leon to *take care of me*. He never wanted any-one to hear what I had to say about that night. He made it look as if I'd shot Michael and I'd run off. Only, he never figured I'd live to tell the truth."

Chase could understand the fear in her eyes. Leon Ridge had pretty much told them a similar story. Funny that Ridge hadn't mentioned that he'd taken Erin out to be shot. Ridge refused to even talk about Erin or her whereabouts. He said he had no idea where Erin was and he didn't care.

When Chase thought about how close she'd come to dying, he asked the obvious. "But you got away?"

"Yes, but only after Leon Ridge put me in a car and took me out to the woods. The minute he dragged me out of the car, I kicked him and used one of my boot heels to dig into his foot. He shot at me and missed. Then I ran and ran and…I've been running since then, hiding out all around Maryland and Virginia." She grabbed at Chase's shirt. "Now do you believe me?"

Chase lifted her up and tugged her into his arms. "Yes, Erin. I believe you. And now that I've heard your side of the story, we'll compare notes and I promise I'm going to do everything I can to clear your name."

Erin nodded. "I've blocked out a lot of that night. Michael wanted to tell me something." She closed her eyes. "He said something. He kept looking over my shoulder and he whispered a word." She gasped and grabbed at Chase's sleeve. "I thought he was trying to say *gone*. That he was telling me I needed to leave. But Chase, what if he was saying a name?"

"Juan," Chase said, the horror in her words chilling him in spite of the hot summer night.

She bobbed her head again, tears falling down her face. "Juan."

Chase drew back, deciding he needed to be honest. "We have Leon Ridge in custody and he told us Jeffries shot Michael, but we found that hard to accept. He claims the shooting was an accident, and that the congressman and he came up with an alibi. He said he shot the congressman to make it look as if an unknown assailant had done it, but he never mentioned that he saw you that night. And he refused to discuss Juan Gomez and the boy's connection to the congressman."

"What? Why didn't you tell me that before now?" Her expression changed, an angry frown clouding her face. "Let me guess. You were waiting to see what I'd tell you, right?"

Chase tried to calm her down. "I had to be careful, Erin. I didn't want to confuse you or upset you."

"You don't believe me after all." She pushed him away. "You probably think I'm lying about him taking me out to kill me."

Chase tugged her back around. "I told you, I believe you. Ridge never told us he'd even seen you. He clams up when we ask about you being there that night."

"That's because Jeffries will have him killed if he says anything else. I'm surprised he said that much, He was there when the congressman decided to pin the whole thing on me, but I got away from Leon. The congressman can't be too happy about that."

"Ridge is obviously the fall guy," Chase explained. "We interviewed the congressman about Juan and the murder, but he denied any involvement. He tried to convince us that Juan was Michael's child."

"That's not possible," Erin exclaimed. "Michael

couldn't have children. It was…always a sore subject between us."

"We know the child isn't Michael's for that very reason. Leon tried to convince us of that, too. We reminded Leon of the opinion piece Michael wrote for one of the local papers, promoting foster care and adoption. The congressman got tripped up in his own lies on that one. He's wanted on corruption charges, but…now we're talking murder, too."

"I asked you to trust me," she reminded him. "You have to trust that I'm telling you the truth. The congressman shot Michael and Michael was trying to tell me why. It's all about that little boy. That makes sense now that I know he's the congressman's son. Leon Ridge planned to kill me, but he won't admit that. And since he failed, Congressman Jeffries will keep sending people to do the job."

"You don't need to convince me anymore," Chase said. "We've all been concerned about your safety. That's why I asked my captain to let me get you somewhere safe for the night."

"Are you sure? Or is that a ploy to take me into custody?"

"Listen, Erin. If we do take you into custody, it will be for your protection. You won't be safe out there on your own. You have to see that."

"I do," she said on a weary voice. "I… I don't know who I can trust, who I can turn to. The congressman obviously always finds me. Jeffries's reach is far and wide."

"So is General Meyer's power," he reminded her. "Let me do my job. Let me help you."

"Thank you," she said on a soft sigh. "I don't have

any choice. If I can't trust you then I'm doomed already."

Chase held his hand to her chin. "I'm here and I'm doing everything I can for you."

She wrapped her arms around his neck and held tight. Chase guided her toward the love seat and pulled her down and back into his arms. He believed Erin's story completely, but…he wasn't sure how to go about proving her innocence to the world. They were fighting a very powerful enemy. He couldn't let his emotions and his involvement with Erin get in the way of his job.

So he held her tight and prayed to God to give him the strength to keep the promise he'd made. And he remembered that with God on his side, he could fight all enemies.

Much later, after he'd sent Erin to bed in the adjoining room, Chase lay awake on the sofa, Valor by his feet, and went back over this case and tried to make a plan of action. First, he needed to let the team know that he'd heard her statement. They'd want to question her, too. Then he needed to go back to Leon Ridge and interrogate him about what had really happened that night and he also wanted to once again interview some of Michael's friends and coworkers. They'd have to go from there, but Chase wasn't sure what might happen.

He was a rookie, only a year into being on the elite handpicked K-9 team. What if they took him off the case? How could he protect her then? Chase was former Secret Service, so he knew how things worked. But he also knew he had a duty to protect Erin, no matter what.

He said a little prayer for guidance and hoped General Meyer would allow him to continue protecting Erin.

She would be in a lot of danger once word got out that she'd been located.

Chase finally gave in to his fatigue and dozed on the uncomfortable little couch for a while. Around 2:00 a.m. Valor alerted with a low growl and Chase was up and holding a weapon toward the French doors out to the upstairs porch. The doors he'd believed no one would breach.

A few minutes later, the intruder broke into the room and found them waiting for him. Chase gave Valor the "Attack" command and Valor leaped into the air and went for the man's throat while Chase circled the culprit.

The man screamed and covered his face, causing Valor to go for his arm. Chase let Valor hold the culprit until he could move in. The man squirmed and writhed in pain, which only made Valor's teeth sink deeper into his bleeding wounds.

"Drop the weapon," Chase said, motioning to the gun the man held in his right hand. Valor backed him up with a low growl and another show of his teeth sinking into the man's left arm. But the man wasn't ready to give in. He pulled the trigger and a shot hit the ceiling with a loud ping. Chase fired back and the man crumbled onto the floor, Valor still holding his arm.

"Release," Chase said. "It's too late for this one, Valor."

When he turned around, Erin was standing in the open door to the other room, her gaze falling across the dead man at Chase's feet.

"You okay?" he asked over his shoulder while he checked the man's pulse and found none.

"Yes," she said behind him, the one word breathless. "That's the man who was chasing me in the woods."

Chase looked back to make sure Erin really was all right. She stood inside the door, wearing the oversize robe, her arms held tightly against her waist.

Chase commanded Valor, "Stay."

Erin advanced a step into the room, her gaze still on the dead assailant. "He was wearing a hat, but I saw his face when I was running away from the hotel. I don't recognize him."

A knock shook the door. "Hey, what's going on in there?"

Janey. Chase gave Erin a warning glance. "Let me handle this."

He opened the door and showed the wide-eyed Janey his badge. After explaining things, he told Janey he was about to make some calls. "I'd appreciate it if you inform the other guests about what's happening and keep them out of the way," he told the frightened woman.

"This won't be good for business," Janey whined. "A dead intruder in the best suite we have. That's a first."

Chase turned to Erin after Janey left and tugged her across the room away from the body. "I need to call this in."

Her eyes narrowed, a flicker of fear deepening them to midnight blue. "You can't take me back. I'll go to jail for something I didn't do."

Chase leaned close, his hand on her elbow. "I don't believe that's gonna happen now. Think about it, Erin. The congressman fled because of the corruption charges and…we now know that Juan Gomez is his son. That's enough to bring him in on murder charges, too, since we have witnesses who say Rosa Gomez was shaking him down for more money right before she died." He also reminded her about Leon Ridge. "We have him in custody and when he hears you're alive and well even though they sent someone to kill you yet again, he's gonna panic."

"But…none of that can help me, Chase. Leon will accuse me since the congressman is pulling his strings. He's too scared to tell the truth and we both know it."

"I'm going to make him tell the truth," Chase said. "Now we have one of Jeffries's thugs breaking in on your room—a room only you and I should have known about. Why would he go to all of this trouble if he isn't trying to kill you?"

"He could convince everyone that he wanted to bring me in to prove I did this."

"But the congressman hasn't told any of us that he was conducting his own investigation and he never fully admitted to seeing you at the scene. We'll question Ridge until he gives us what we need."

"And in the meantime, what happens to me?" she asked.

Chase glanced back toward the dead guy and then turned to her again. "In the meantime, I'm going to make sure you stay safe."

Erin sat on the sofa and watched as law-enforcement people tramped back and forth in what had started out as a beautiful suite in a quiet country bed-and-breakfast. She'd been questioned and prodded and interrogated and analyzed to the point that she was no longer coherent. All she wanted right now was a soft bed and sleep. Lots of sleep without nightmares or visions of people chasing her through the woods.

"How you holding up?" Chase asked, sitting down beside her for a brief moment. Valor had stayed by her side while his human partner did his job and filed his own report.

"I'm okay," she said. Then she shook her head. "No, that's not true. I'm tired, scared and worried that I'll be hauled away the minute they're done here. Poor Janey is probably afraid they'll take her in, too. I think every branch of law enforcement sent several representatives to gawk at me and get me to confess to anything and everything. I'll probably be blamed for Leon Ridge's confession, too." She lifted her hand toward the window. "Not to mention the reporters already gathering out there. I'm the topic of the day."

"Janey can use all of this as PR," Chase said, obviously trying to make her smile. "She's handling the reporters with cookies and coffee. I don't even want to think about what she's telling them. She'll have gawkers driving by for weeks."

"At least someone will profit from my notoriety," Erin replied with a frown.

Chase touched his hand to hers in a quick gesture. "It's going to be all right. Oh, by the way, your father's on his way, too."

Erin moaned and held a hand in her hair. "I was hoping I'd see him back at his town house in DC. He shouldn't drive all the way out here. We're at least two hours away from the city."

"He's bringing lawyers," Chase said, his eyes full of understanding and sympathy. "I tried—"

"—to talk him out of it," she finished. "I know how that goes." Then she turned serious. "Will I have to be arraigned or post bail or whatever comes next?"

Chase's smile was soft and swift. "Hold on, Sherlock. You aren't going to be charged with anything right now. But you will be questioned."

She pushed at her hair. "Again?"

"And again," he said, his eyes holding hers. "You are innocent until proven guilty, remember? Leon Ridge did tell us that the congressman *accidentally* shot his son."

"I am innocent," she said, hoping he really did believe her. "But Chase…if it's all over the news that… I've been brought in, what do you think Congressman Jeffries will do?"

Chase glanced around to where Captain Gavin McCord stood talking to two FBI agents. They'd already taken the dead man away, but Erin wondered what they would do with her. Did Chase really think he could stop this steamroller?

"Chase?"

He turned back to her. "The congressman will come after you."

Erin tried to ignore the shudder creeping down her spine. "He'll be in a panic knowing Leon's been arrested and that another of his minions is now dead. He still wants *me* dead. I can't see that changing. I think it'll only get worse."

"He's running out of options so he's getting desperate," Chase said. "Look, let's get done here and…if you don't want to go back to your place or to your father's house, you can come home with me."

"That won't be necessary, Officer Zachary."

Erin cringed and turned, recognizing her father's stern voice. She shot Chase a glance and saw the dare in his green eyes. Getting up, she hurried to her father before Chase said anything. "Dad."

"Baby." Her father pulled her close and for a moment, Erin felt like a little girl again. Tall with hair that had once been dark brown but was now mostly a silvery white, Senator Preston Eagleton had always been a handsome man. And right now, with the scent of expensive cigars and spicy aftershave engulfing her, Erin felt safe again. It was good to be back in her father's strong arms. Her dad drew back to look at her. "Are you all right?"

"I am now," she said, tears pricking at her eyes. "I'm sorry I worried you all these months."

Her father looked her over. "My doctor will meet us and give you a thorough checkup after we move you out to our house. I thought you'd have more privacy out from the city."

"That's not necessary," she said, shaking her head at the thought of heading to her father's vast country estate. "I'm tired and I have a few bug bites, but—"

"My daughter, hiding out in the woods." Her father gave her a harsh glance. "Why didn't you call me, Erin?"

"I had my reasons," she said, "and I don't want to talk about all of that right now."

FIVE

Seeing the formidable Washington attorney her father kept on retainer, Erin's pulse escalated. "Do you think I killed Congressman Jeffries, Daddy?"

"Or course not," her father retorted. "I only brought my lawyer with me as a precaution." He glanced at Chase. "I've had my own team working on finding you since General Meyer didn't want to divulge her K-9 team's investigation with me."

"For your own safety and protection, sir," Chase said, stepping forward.

He held out a hand and her father shook it, but Erin saw the gesture was out of politeness and nothing more. "I know how to take care of myself and…my daughter," her father said to Chase. "Now, if you're done with her…"

"Erin, what do you want to do?" Chase asked, his tone firm and sure. "We can take you to a safe house right now."

Torn between staying secure near Chase and wanting to visit with her father, she glanced between the both of them. "I'll be okay, Chase," she finally said. "That is, if I'm free to go."

Her father's lawyer stepped forward. "Erin, I'm so glad you're all right. Let me go and talk to Captain McCord and the other officers and we'll have you out of here in a few minutes."

Chase gave her a reassuring look. "I'll speak to Gavin, too." He leaned close. "I'll explain things to him. We need to know you'll be safe."

Her father frowned after Chase hurried away. "What was that all about?"

Erin didn't want to argue with her father so soon after seeing him again, but she had to be honest. "I'm still in danger, Daddy."

Her father glanced around as if someone in the room might be after her. "Oh, and how's that?"

"I didn't kill Michael, but…I know who did."

Shocked, her father pulled her close. "What are you saying, Erin?"

"I'm not sure, but I think Congressman Jeffries will keep sending people after me."

"Are you suggesting that Harland Jeffries is trying to kill you?"

"I *know* he's trying to kill me," she retorted, wondering if her own father doubted her. "That's why I had to go into hiding. I saw him murder Michael."

Her father's features were schooled in a calm facade, but she'd seen the disbelief in his eyes. "All the more reason to get you away from the city and home where we can talk in private."

Erin glanced over at Chase. "I'll go with you if they let me leave, but I might have to go to Capitol K-9 headquarters for more questioning."

"Not tonight," her father replied. "You need to be checked over and you need to rest." He shot a condemning glance toward Chase. "After all, he didn't do a very good job of protecting you."

Erin had learned a thing or two out there on her own. One being that if she didn't stand up to people, she'd never learn how to survive anything. "Dad, Chase did more than protect me tonight. He's been searching for me since the night Michael died. He found me and he saved my life. You might consider that before you dismiss him completely."

Her father looked suitably chastised, his gaze moving from her to behind her. When Erin looked around, Chase was standing close enough to have heard what she'd said.

He gave her a look of appreciation then turned to her father. "You're free to go, Erin," he said, his eyes on Senator Eagleton. "Sir, we're depending on you to keep her close to home for now since we'll need to interrogate Erin again. Captain McCord will send some officers to help patrol your estate." Then he glanced back at Erin. "I'll come by first thing in the morning to check on you."

"That won't be—" the senator began, then he changed his tune. "Don't be too early, son. She needs a good night's sleep." He reached out his hand to Chase. "And…thank you for finding my daughter."

Back at headquarters early the next morning, Chase was questioned by everyone from the president's special in-house security chief, General Meyer, to Metro Police Detective David Delvecchio and Secret Service Agent Dan Calvert. All of the interagency big guns wanted in on this one. And his boss, Captain Gavin McCord, wanted a play-by-play of everything leading up to Chase finding Erin and what happened afterward.

"Someone was chasing her when I found her so I had to make the choice of protecting Erin instead of going after the perpetrator. After that, it was late and she was tired, but I called you right away to report I had her," he repeated for about the tenth time. "I was pretty sure we were being tailed so I took her to the inn until morning. But the tail obviously followed us since the assailant showed up where we were staying."

"She could have easily escaped again," Captain Mc-Cord pointed out with an intimidating frown. "I should have ordered you to bring her in right away."

That same frown shadowed just about every face on the entire Capitol K-9 team. Metro Police Detective Delvecchio cleared his throat in what could have been a skeptical snort. The cynical detective had cooperated, but he hadn't been happy with having to share information with the K-9 team. Captain McCord had managed to get past that, at least.

"She didn't run," Chase retorted. "Valor was on alert and besides, she was so exhausted she fell asleep as soon as she went to bed. I took her statement and I caught yet another man trying to kill her."

"Or at least breaking into her room," General Meyer said, her vivid blue eyes nailing Chase to his chair. But he'd also seen a hint of compassion in those all-knowing eyes. The general was a smart cookie and this team had her heart. Maybe she'd cut Chase some slack since he'd been working this case since the night they'd found Michael Jeffries dead and the congressman wounded.

"Yes, you did bring in our key witness," Captain McCord said. "Good work." He scrolled through his phone. "I'm waiting to hear if we have an identity on your intruder."

Chase hoped that identity would give them another piece to the puzzle.

"I have reason to believe Erin is still in danger," he said. "I'd like permission to be put on her protection team."

"You'll continue this investigation," McCord said in a tone would brook no argument. "I know you were once close to Erin, but Chase, you're *too* close now and besides, Erin will be safe with her father out at his estate. He understands she's a person of interest and possible witness in this case so his lawyers are advising him to keep her close. We'll send some of our people to patrol the perimeters, too."

"Agreed," Chase said, figuring now was not the time to argue. "Where do you want me?"

"I want you to try to get in touch with some of Michael Jeffries's friends. Ask them again if he seemed upset about the Gomez boy, find out if they talked to him that day. We've questioned a lot of people already, but now that we have Erin Eagleton's statement, we start back at square one. If you hear anything about Erin and Michael having words or acting in any unusual way, you'd better report it immediately." His gaze moved around the room. "Leon Ridge left out everything Miss Eagleton has told us. I'll be questioning him on that, too."

Chase wondered if the captain was even now still willing to vouch for Congressman Jeffries. Maybe he was also too close to this case to see what was obvious. The do-good congressman had fooled a lot of people, including Captain McCord. The captain's former mentor needed to come forward and face the music so they could all get on with things. So Erin could get her life back, at least.

General Meyer continued the conversation. "And talk to Cassie Danvers again." She glanced at Gavin as if daring him to disapprove since Cassie and the captain had become a couple after the foster home had been vandalized and almost burned down. They were now engaged to be married. "You can find her at the temporary safe house where Gavin placed the All Our Kids foster children and house mother Cassie when they were in danger. She might remember something about Michael coming by to see the little boy that week."

"Captain?" Chase waited to verify the approval since the captain seemed unsure about Chase's motives right now.

"She's at the safe house," Captain McCord said. "She's been through a lot, but Cassie's strong. If anyone can help us, she will."

Chase itched to call Erin, but he had his orders, and at least this footwork would keep him busy. Besides, maybe he did need to distance himself from her so he could stick to the facts. Hadn't he been trained to study the evidence and keep his personal judgments to himself? But when he thought about what Erin had told him, Chase went with his instincts and remembered the captain had commended him several times on doing just that. Chase had always believed in Erin's innocence and now the facts were beginning to back him up.

Capitol K-9 Unit member Adam Donovan stood in a corner of the briefing room with his partner, Ace. The big Doberman's head moved from side to side while Adam, a former FBI agent, didn't seem to move at all.

Chase gave Valor a silent command and walked over to greet Adam. Valor needed a good rest and so did Chase. He hadn't slept very well last night and this would be another long day of work.

Adam nodded as he approached. "Tough morning, Rookie?"

"You got it," Chase replied. "I'm being given grunt work to keep me away from Erin."

Adam gave him an understanding smile since he'd fallen in love with Lana Gomez, the sister of the late Rosa Gomez, who'd been Congressman Jeffries's housekeeper and the mother of his toddler son. "Well, you did tell us right up front that you and Erin had a past. Captain doesn't forget things like that, you know."

"Yep. Full disclosure—that's my game," Chase replied. "I'm worried about her, though. I think Jeffries will try to come after her again."

"So you believe her story?" Adam asked on a low tone.

Chase had racked his brain over this and his gut kept coming back to the same conclusion. "I do, yes. Erin has always been honest and I can't see why that would change. Her story supports what Ridge told us. He just left out the part about her being there, of course. She's been through the worst, Adam."

Adam lifted off the wall. "Then, man, you gotta follow your gut like the captain always says. We train our animals to do just that, right?"

"Good point," Chase replied. "Meantime, I'm going to pound the pavement to get to the truth."

Erin woke with a start. For a minute, she thought she was still out there in the dark, running for her life, and a sick panic set in. But when she blinked and sat up, she realized she was back in the room she remembered so well, her room in her father's Maryland house miles away from Washington, DC. Her father had been shot right here in the backyard, near the gazebo. One of his favorite spots since her parents used to dine out there during good weather.

Thank goodness he'd survived. He surprised Erin when he told her that her cousin Selena had come to eat lunch with him the day an attempt had been made on his life. Erin was happy that her father had reached out to Selena, since he and Selena's late mother had a rocky past. But Selena had been in danger, too.

Was someone determined to kill everyone in her family?

Would they go after Chase, too?

In her mind, she was now about a thousand memories away from Chase.

Did you expect him to follow you out here?

Chase had done his job and brought her back to face her accusers. Was he one of them?

No. Chase believed in her. She'd seen it in his eyes and in the way he'd protected her and trusted her last night. But what about now? They had a confession from Leon, true. But Jeffries wouldn't like being betrayed and that was probably why Leon refused to confirm that Erin had been at the murder scene. Jeffries thought he could pin Michael's death on her, but now she had become a credible witness instead.

Because of Gavin McCord's original devotion to Congressman Jeffries, the Capitol K-9 team would pursue this case until the bitter end. She prayed they'd find Jeffries before he made another move toward her.

Michael deserved justice.

Tears pricked at her eyes as she remembered Michael lying there, so still, his life blood running out of his body while his own father did nothing to save him.

The house phone rang, causing her to jump. When her father's secretary told Erin that her cousin Selena Barrow was on the private line, Erin took the phone receiver and got out of bed to go over to the mint-green chaise longue by the big window overlooking the backyard.

"I've tried all morning to get through," Selena said when she heard Erin's voice. "I'm so glad you're all right, Erin. Nicholas and I have been so worried."

"Who's Nicholas?" Erin asked after thanking Selena.

Selena's light laughter surprised Erin. "It's a long story, but…he's Nicholas Cole—a member of the Capitol K-9 team who's on White House detail along with his partner, Max. We…uh…met when someone broke into General Meyer's office—"

Erin had briefly talked to General Meyer late last night or maybe it had been early this morning. They'd met at several Washington functions and she liked the stoic older woman. "Wait, she's the head of the K-9 team, right? She's the boss."

"Yes, and she has a long title, but she's also a retired four-star general so everyone calls her General," Selena went on. "Anyway, someone also ransacked my office at the White House that same day."

"I am behind," Erin replied, remembering how she'd tried to draw her less fortunate cousin into her circle of friends, but her father had frowned on that. He'd never forgiven Selena's alcoholic mother—his deceased sister—for always calling him for help through the years. She'd embarrassed him one time too many in public, so he'd distanced himself from his only sister and his niece. But Erin liked Selena and wanted to rekindle their relationship. "Why did someone break into your office?"

"They took my electronic notebook," Selena replied. "The one I've kept for months…on you."

Erin's heart clanked against her ribs. "Why me, Selena?"

"I believe you're innocent," Selena said with such conviction it brought fresh tears to Erin's eyes. "I tried to do whatever I could to help prove that, but I finally had to back off and let the authorities do their thing, including the entire Capitol K-9 team. Nicholas can't tell me much, but he says things are looking up for you." Selena's soft sigh lifted across the silence. "I know you didn't kill Michael, Erin. And if I have my way, I'll make sure the whole Capitol K-9 team and everyone up to the president himself feels the same way. This team is amazing. They'll keep hammering that shady Leon Ridge until he tells them the whole story. The human team members are about as tenacious as their canine counterparts. Like a dog with a bone."

Erin didn't know what to say. Over the years, she and Selena had lost touch and had seen each other again three years ago at Selena's mom's funeral. After that, they'd tried to have lunch here and there, but they'd truly reconnected late last year when Erin had spotted Selena at the White House during a charity event. But it hadn't been easy trying to get together, mainly because Erin had gotten caught up in the whirlwind world of Washington, keeping up with the Eagleton Foundation and also maintaining a good facade so her father would never have to be involved in any scandals. The irony of that was not lost on her. They were both up to their eyeballs in this particular scandal.

And yet even after the way Erin's father had treated Selena, her cousin had believed in her. "I'm sorry my dad and I haven't stayed in touch with you," she said.

"Oh, but your dad and I have grown close," Selena replied. "I was out at the house when he got shot and I saw him in the hospital later and he asked me to forgive him. Then I sat with him at the town house once he came home. Everything is forgiven, Erin." At Erin's silence, she added, "Everything, okay?"

"Thank you," Erin said again, her voice husky with emotion. "I'm so glad to hear that and I hope we can see each other soon. I'm kind of under house arrest right now. Hard to get away."

"Don't try," Selena retorted. "The press has even begun calling me for sound bites. But…I'm *not* biting. You're in the safest place you can be right now. Your dad hired some serious security after our scare in the garden."

Erin reluctantly agreed then asked, "So…you and Officer Cole are…close?"

Selena let out a sigh that sounded contented. "Yes. Very close. As in—engaged. We hope to get married soon."

"That's wonderful news," Erin replied, thoughts of Chase circling through her tattered brain. "I wish you the best."

"You'll be at the wedding," Selena said on a sure note. "I hope you'll agree to be one of my bridesmaids."

Erin wasn't so confident. "I'd be honored. I hope I can do that."

Selena said, "You will. We have to have faith." Before Erin could respond, she added, "And by the way, the news reports are saying you were brought in by Chase Zachary. Is this the same Chase Zachary you dated in high school?"

"Yes, it's him," Erin replied, wondering if she'd ever hear from Chase again. And wondering why she'd confided in Selena about that. Not that she minded Selena knowing. It was just hard to accept that Chase was back in her life in such a strange way—bringing her in under a cloud of suspicion. "He found me, somehow, and he saved my life the other night."

Selena gasped. "We need to talk more, but I have to go. And I know you're exhausted. I just wanted you to know—if you need me for anything, and I mean anything, call me at this number."

Erin grabbed a pen and notepad and took down Selena's cell number. "Thank you again, Selena. I can't tell you how much this means to me."

"Hey, we're family," Selena replied. "Remember that."

SIX

Erin hung up and stared out the window, but she didn't notice the manicured yard or the perfectly trimmed trees and shrubs or even the lush woods beyond the grounds. She couldn't believe she was back here after all these years. Or that her cousin had tried to come to her defense.

Dressing quickly, she decided she wouldn't hide in her room all day. Too many memories were crashing down around her, many of them involving Chase. They had been teenagers then, and now they'd been thrust back together as adults. She should have run away from him last night, too. But…when he'd tugged her close and told her everything would be okay, she'd believed him.

He'd told her that once before, too, and that hadn't turned out so well. He hadn't trusted her enough to believe she'd come back to him after her trip to Africa the summer of their high school graduation. Erin had had every intention of coming home to Chase so they could plan their college agendas and later…their wedding. But he'd been so angry at her for going in the first place, he'd broken things off.

"This will save you having to do it," he'd said. "We

both know we'll never make it. We're too different, from two different worlds."

She'd left, heartbroken but determined to win him back come fall. But Chase had refused to even talk to her.

Their high school sweetheart love affair had ended all too soon. And she still regretted letting that happen.

Would a murder case that had the whole nation talking bring them back together, or just tear them apart again?

Erin didn't know what to think about that. She prayed that soon all of the facts could be made public and that she could go back to her life and the responsibility of running the Eagleton Foundation. And maybe if nothing else…she and Chase could be friends.

"He's sure lawyered up."

Chase stood outside the interrogation room where they were holding Leon Ridge, thinking the same thing his friend and fellow officer Nicholas Cole had just stated. "Yeah, but he's lying and we all know it."

Captain McCord came out of the room, looking grim. "He claims he doesn't know what happened to the murder weapon," McCord said, a hand slicing through his dark brown hair. "A small-caliber handgun was used to kill Michael Jeffries. But he won't budge much on anything else, especially regarding Erin Eagleton and her missing car. Says he didn't move Erin's car, but he's suddenly insisting the congressman told him *later* that the shooter was Erin Eagleton and that's why he went after her. But the congressman told us he didn't see the shooter." The captain put his hands on his hips, his expression full of fatigue. "Leon claims he only confessed to help out the congressman, who's like a father to him. He must think Jeffries will help him out of this jam, but I don't see that happening. We seem to have conflicting reports here."

"It makes sense that Ridge shot both of them and is now trying to finger Erin as the shooter," Chase said. "But she says she walked up on the congressman and Michael arguing, and that the congressman held the gun to Michael's stomach. She thinks it was an accident, but the congressman wouldn't help save his own son."

McCord rubbed a hand down his five o'clock shadow. "So Ridge might be willing to take the rap for the congressman or he's just buying time, maybe giving the congressman more time to get wherever he thinks he's going."

"Ridge won't talk anymore now that the fancy lawyer is back," Chase said, disgusted. "And can I just guess who managed to send that lawyer?"

McCord glared at him. "Congressman Jeffries?"

"You got it. Probably to intimidate Ridge, if nothing else."

"I agree with you, Zachary," McCord said with a grudging admiration and a solid acceptance. "But we need more evidence. So I suggest you get back out there."

"Yes, sir." Chase sent Nicholas a raised-eyebrow glance then silently commanded Valor to "Come."

The next few hours were spent calling Michael Jeffries's friends and coworkers and, sometimes, finding them in person. Chase had left his contact cards with half a dozen people. He got a call from McCord that the man he'd shot at the country inn was a low-level hit man who had a long criminal history. But he'd never talk now and they didn't have any leads on who had sent him.

At around sundown, his cell phone rang again. Chase had just stopped to grab a bite and he was still parked, with Valor in the back eating his own dinner. When he answered, he was surprised to hear Cassie Danvers's voice. He'd left her a message earlier since she still ran the All Our Kids group foster home that for now was being housed in a safe location out of the city.

"You wanted to speak to me?" Cassie asked. She sounded breathless and he could hear voices in the background. He had to admire the woman. She had a tough job trying to keep several children of all ages contained and safe.

"Yes. Thanks for returning my call." Chase crushed his cell phone between his shoulder and ear, and scrolled through his paper notebook. "I wanted to ask you a few questions regarding Michael Jeffries. Specifically, if you or anyone on your staff talked with him the week or so before he died."

"I already told the DC police and the FBI that I didn't talk with Michael during that time and as far as I know, no one on my staff did either. But you have to realize, Michael and the congressman both stopped by the foster home a lot."

"Could you check again?" Chase said. "It's really important. Several of his friends say he was upset right before his death, allegedly that he'd found out Juan Gomez might be related to him."

"And we've established that," Cassie said, her tone kind if not weary. "I don't recall talking to him, but my assistant, Virginia Johnson, might have. She sometimes filters visitors while I'm dealing with one of the kids."

"Could I possibly speak to her?" Chase asked. "I need any information that can help establish that Michael was extremely upset and that he went to his father's house to possibly confront him about Juan Gomez."

"I'll tell Virginia you'd like to question her—maybe tomorrow morning." When he heard a crash, she said, "Look, I can't talk right now, but I'll call you soon, okay?"

Chase ended the call with about as much information as he'd started with this morning. How could he prove Erin was telling the truth if he couldn't find one person to corroborate her story? Deciding to call it a day and take himself off duty for a while, he headed out toward Senator Eagleton's house to check on things and hopefully visit with Erin for a couple of minutes. He exited the interstate and cruised along the scenic country road dotted with huge homes. He'd never fit in with Erin's world, and that was one reason he'd let her go.

He'd never been good enough for her.

But he had to be good at his job in order to save her.

Erin glanced up to see Chase and Valor walking toward where she sat with a guard nearby on the back veranda, watching storm clouds gather over the horizon. She knew this was serious by the way the other three guards her father had hired accompanied him. The stoic guards were always dressed in black, complete with bulletproof Kevlar vests, and they carried radios and semiautomatic rifles. Similar to Chase, but not nearly as comforting.

"Hi," she said when he approached. Valor was with

him, so she waved the overbearing guards away. "What are you doing here?"

She hadn't seen him since two nights ago when he'd turned and walked away after her father had come to the inn to insist she come home with him.

"Hi." He motioned to two wrought iron chairs. "Mind if we sit and talk?"

"Have a seat." She couldn't ignore the relief washing through her after seeing him again, but from the brooding expression on his face, she dreaded what he'd come here to say to her. He waited for her to sit and then ordered Valor to do the same. The furry dog curled up between them, his dark eyes following Erin.

She held her hands fisted at her side. "You must have a really good reason for coming all the way out here to see me."

He glanced around the yard, his gaze landing on the shimmering pool. "I'm not here in an official capacity. Just wanted to make sure you're okay."

Erin started to protest until she noticed the dark circles of fatigue hovering around his eyes. His green gaze danced over her with concern, but the dark clouds hid his face in silent shadows. Chase had to be every bit as tired as she was.

"I tried to argue with myself to stay away," he said. "But I think being here with you might be good for both of us. I needed a break."

The edge in his voice caught at her. "Do you still have doubts about me?"

The split second of hesitation before he answered told Erin the truth, but she let him speak.

"I have never doubted you." He slanted his head.

"Can't we just…talk? I needed to see you, Erin. And it has nothing to do with this investigation."

"Or maybe it has everything to do with this investigation."

Chase stood and came to kneel in front of her. "Listen. I have to go on facts. I don't mean to doubt you, but this is a big case and we need to have everything in order. Even your testimony. Because if we capture Jeffries, you will be a key witness in what happened the night of the murder at his house."

Seeing the sincerity and concern in his eyes, Erin tried to relax. "I understand. You have a job to do. I want this to be done right, too. It just seems as if I keep coming up against a wall with every attempt to make things right."

"It's more than just doing my job," he said, his hands over hers. "I want to protect you and stand by you, too."

And he'd been trying to do that at every turn. When she'd been the one doubting him and everyone else at every turn.

"I'm sorry." Erin's gaze met his. "And I'm being rude, trying to pick a fight with you. You're right. I need a break, too. Since I've been back, it's been crazy. Reporters, officers, lawyers, you name it. I've had calls from all of them. Thank you for coming."

Chase did a neck roll and Valor half rose in high hopes they were going into action. "It's nice to just sit in the shade and enjoy the day. I'm tired."

"I get that," she said, the warmth of his hands bringing her comfort. "I can make us a grilled cheese sandwich."

"Mmm. Sounds good."

She moved an inch closer. Pushing at her short ponytail, she said, "Since doing things on my own hasn't helped me all that much, I think I have to trust in the people who've tried to protect me, no matter what. That's you and your team, Chase. And I have to trust in God and pray that with His grace, my innocence will be clear once and for all."

"We can all agree on that."

When Chase signaled Valor, the canine got up and came to sit by Erin. She reached down and petted the big dog and gave Chase a thankful smile. "At least Valor seems to like me."

"He's one smart animal," Chase said, grinning.

There was so much between them. She wanted him to know that she now understood God's love in her life. They could both apply that to their life together and, maybe, at least be friends again. But she worried that she'd never have any friends at all.

Chase got up and pulled her to her feet. "Hey, don't go down any gloomy roads, okay?"

She smiled up at him. "In spite of those summer storms brewing in the sky?"

He glanced behind them. "A good night to stay in and pop popcorn and watch one of those sappy movies women like, right?"

"Right." She reached for his hand. "My dad's working late, so other than the four horsemen over there, we're alone."

Chase tugged her close. "Well, we can sit here and watch the storm roll in. Together. Okay?"

Erin nodded but resisted touching a hand to his cheek. "I'd love that."

Meantime, she would pray that it wasn't too late for them to have a second chance.

* * *

The next evening, Chase drove through the countryside, remembering how much they'd reconnected last night. A couple of hours of catching up and talking had helped him to relax and refocus on this investigation. Erin was still the sweet, smart girl he remembered. Only now she was a grown woman, a strong woman who wanted justice for Michael Jeffries.

So he'd been going back over any contacts who might help him figure out something to connect the dots on this case.

When his phone rang again, he hoped Cassie Danvers had thought of something along those lines. He still hadn't heard back from her.

But it wasn't Cassie on the line.

"Chase, it's Erin."

"Erin? What is it?"

"I…someone's in our house. I mean, I saw someone in the garden, down by the pool. A prowler."

Chase gunned the truck and headed out into traffic. "Where are your father and the guards?"

"My father had a commitment in the city and I don't know where the guards are. They're not responding to my calls. The whole house is quiet."

"I'll be there in a few minutes. Meantime, take your phone and hide. Do you hear me, Erin? Hide."

"Okay. Can I stay on the phone with you?"

He warred with how to answer that, his heart slipping and sliding in the same way his truck was skidding through traffic. "Call 911. Stay on the line with them, okay?"

"Someone's coming," she said. "Chase?"

"Stay with me, then," he shouted, the burger he'd

eaten too fast congealing in his stomach. "I'm on the way. Just hang on. I'll put you on hold while I call this in."

"No. Don't…just hurry. I hear footsteps."

Chase didn't dare hang up now. "Erin? Erin, are you there?"

No answer. The connection was abruptly cut off.

Erin listened, her breath coming in quick gasps, as someone moved through the rooms downstairs. Where were the armed guards her father had hired to patrol the yard and house? Where were the officers Captain McCord had sent out to the estate?

Since she'd tossed her cell phone long ago, she'd been carrying the cordless phone around her room all day. Now it had gone dead. The backup battery must have run down.

But when she hurried to the cradle to check, fear coursed through her veins. It didn't matter if she put the phone back to the cradle since someone had cut the phone lines right along with the electricity and, apparently, the state-of-the-art alarm system that her father had promised would keep her safe.

Chase is on the way, she kept telling herself while she locked her bedroom door and then searched for a viable weapon. He'd alert some of the team members patrolling the grounds, too.

Weary that she was once again in danger, Erin refused to give in or give up. She was home now and… after months of being isolated and surviving with her wits only, she wasn't about to go down without a fight when she was so close to finding hope again. So when she heard the footsteps moving up the spiral staircase toward the second floor, she found her way by moonlight and hurried to the big closet that still held a lot of her old clothes and shoes, and groped in the dark for anything she could use as a means of protection.

When her hand hit on an old tennis racket, Erin's heart stalled and restarted in a sputtering gulp of air. It wasn't much, but it could hurt if she remembered to swing it as if she were serving a ball to an opponent. Then she pushed boxes and storage bins up against the closet door as a barrier between her and whoever came after her. If she could hit the attacker over the head or trip him at least, she'd be able to run.

Crouching in a corner behind some boxes and old boots, she prayed that no spidery creatures were living inside her closet, and that whoever was coming up those stairs wouldn't find her before Chase and the police did.

He'd call for backup. That much she knew. He'd have Valor with him, too. And that smart and capable animal would rush to save her. All she had to do was protect herself before the intruder found her. But she could hear each creak of the house, and she knew every board on those old stairs. The intruder would be here before she could find a way to escape.

Erin took deep, calming breaths and willed herself to become small and invisible. She'd played hide-and-seek as a child, but she'd never imagined she'd have to hide from a real culprit who might do her harm or finish her off for good.

But she'd learned something since she'd left life as she'd known it and become a hermit. She'd found a strength she never knew existed and…she'd found her faith again.

How much longer can I live like this, dear Lord?

Please help me to find a way out of this. You know my heart. You know I didn't kill Michael and You know who's behind all of this. Help me, Lord.

Her silent prayer looped through her head in a hundred different ways while the seconds ticked off like a time bomb about to explode. With her sweaty hands gripping the aged handle of the once-expensive tennis racket, she envisioned what she would do when that door opened.

And then she heard the crash of her bedroom door as it burst back against the wall. Someone was now inside her bedroom. Thinking she should have tried to make it out of the house, Erin centered her thoughts so she could use every self-defense tactic she'd ever learned. She'd been able to save herself several times because she refused to be a victim.

That was one thing her mother, Gayle, had taught her.

"You are strong and capable, Erin. Never play the victim. Never blame your troubles on someone else. God will see you through. He will give you strength, but in this world, you have to learn to stand up for yourself and your beliefs."

Her mother's words, spoken in such a cultured, sure way, made Erin sit up and prepare herself for the worst. She'd lost her mother years ago when she was in middle school. Thinking of her now gave Erin the strength she needed.

Holding her breath, she slid up against the hanging clothes, the scents of a thousand old perfumes surrounding her in a cloying grip. The door handle shook and rattled, causing Erin to lift the racket up to shield her face.

And then she heard sirens off in the distance, heard

the squeal of tires in the driveway below. Gasping in a long breath of air, she moved forward, the tennis racket her weapon.

The doorknob jiggled again. Was he going to try to kill her before someone found him?

Erin stepped behind some old coats, sweat pouring down her back, her T-shirt clinging to her rib cage. When the door was shoved open, she heard a man cursing and heaving a groan.

And then, all of her barriers were pushed aside and he was inside the closet. Erin almost screamed, but she waited…one, two, three heartbeats.

A dog's angry bark stopped the invader, who was now only a foot away from her. She could smell the foulness of his sweat, could hear his low curses and his hurried breathing.

Then the man turned and ran out of the closet, out of the room and down the stairs.

Erin clung to the tennis racket and hurried out from under the weight of her old clothes. Valor barked and snarled as the front door of the house was shoved open. The big animal's growls and barks continued while Erin ran to the door of her bedroom. She heard another door slamming somewhere deep inside the house and guessed the intruder had gone out the kitchen or garage door.

"Erin?"

Chase!

"In here," she called, her whole body beginning to shake. "I'm in here, Chase. He…he got away."

SEVEN

More police officers nosing around, more K-9 officers searching the woods behind her father's estate, more questions coming at her from all directions. More tense glances from Chase as he updated her father, the DC police and the ever-present FBI and Secret Service. Maybe now at least, they'd all believe someone wanted her dead.

Erin sat on a couch in the formal living room, shock and exhaustion trying to take her under, trying to drown her. Valor was stationed at her feet. They'd brought the dog in a few minutes ago. But the others were still out there looking. Out there searching in this never-ending nightmare.

They'd never catch these people. She might not ever be completely free. Not until they found Congressman Jeffries at least. But he'd put his politician's spin on this. She could rest only when they had his full confession.

Chase's clear emerald-green eyes held her, lifted her back up. He came and sat down beside her, his expression pinched with fatigue. "Just got word. We lost him in the woods near a creek."

Erin nodded, unable to speak until she took a drink

of water. Holding the glass with both hands so she wouldn't shake, she said, "I…I didn't get a good look at his face, but he was tall and dressed in black. Oh, wait, I've already told you that."

Chase gave her a patient smile. "It's okay if you repeat things. It only means you saw what you saw, but you might add details as you remember."

"I'm glad my father wasn't here," she said. Casting a glance toward where her dad stood with two officers, she let out a held breath. "The guards my father hired—"

"One was knocked out and one stabbed," Chase replied on a grim note. "They've both been taken to the hospital and we hear they'll be okay. We questioned one of the other two. He got blindsided, too."

"Didn't we all?"

"Yes. Whoever did this knew his way around this place. He waited until our two officers made the rounds and when they walked down to the gate to do a sweep, he came in the back way and cut the electricity, phone lines and security. Then he attacked the first guards to come up on him and got away from the one guard who came up on him late." He leaned close. "I want to make sure this doesn't happen again. We need to take you to an undisclosed location."

"Selena," she said, her heart sputtering. "She said to call her if I need help."

Chase drew back, concern flashing across his face. "Your cousin? I don't think that's a good idea since she had some trouble at her place a couple of months ago." He remembered all of the details since he'd been following anything that might involve Erin. "She actually got close to your father after we questioned him about another case that Michael had been working on. After he was shot, she stayed in his town house and helped him plan a gala."

Erin felt a rush of surprise mixed with a heavy guilt when she remembered Selena telling her the same thing. "I've caused both of them so much trouble. I'm glad Selena was there when Dad needed her, and I don't want to put her in danger. She's been through a lot on my behalf and she is planning her wedding. Maybe involving her is a bad idea."

He sat there doing the Chase thing in his head, calculating, analyzing, deciphering. He lowered his head, scratched Valor behind his ear. "Yep, a lot of engagements happening these days." Then he gave Erin a direct green-eyed stare that spoke of things neither of them was ready to say.

"I think we'd better just take you to a safe house."

"Yes. I don't need to bother Selena."

He nodded. "Maybe you and Selena can have a long phone visit. The entire team will help protect you." He touched her hand for the briefest of seconds. "And I'll be around."

"Will your captain agree to that?"

"I'll convince him."

She had no doubt he'd do just that. Chase had always been stubborn and sure, but she sensed a need in him—a need to prove himself, to help a friend, to do this job.

"Should I call Selena?" she offered.

"Let me…clear this with the higher-ups. Even phone calls can be monitored for your location."

Erin gazed around the crowded room. "Might want to clear it with my father, too."

He didn't look worried about that. "I'll make him understand that the estate is no longer safe for you."

Their eyes held, memories pulling her to the surface, holding her tight. "Thank you."

Then her father came over, his expression full of rage. "I can't believe this happened. What good is security if it doesn't work?" Giving Erin an apologetic glance, he said, "I'm so sorry, honey. I thought any attacks against me were long over...after Carly Jones was arrested."

Erin shook her head. Her father had explained how his chief of staff had been taking bribes from lobbyists for years. When someone tried to blackmail her, she tried to frame Selena for her crimes. "I'm so sorry I wasn't here with you, Daddy."

Her father held her close. "Well, you're here now, darlin'."

"Chase is moving me to a new location. Undisclosed," she replied, hoping her father wouldn't fight this. "I won't put you in danger anymore."

The senator's expression changed from sympathetic to furious again. "I don't think—"

"It's my decision, Daddy."

Chase stood, his fists tight. He looked as if he were in fight mode. Valor's ears went up.

Her father's gaze moved between them in a silent power struggle. "What's the plan?" he finally asked Chase.

Chase seemed to relax and Valor went back down on his belly, but kept his head up. "I've got to clear a few things with my captain and General Meyer, but... I think it best if we hide Erin until we can locate Congressman Jeffries."

"Where?" the senator asked.

"I'd rather not let anyone outside of the team know," Erin said before Chase could speak. She stood, straightened. "The fewer who know, the better," she added. "But I'll keep in touch, Daddy. I promise."

"I don't like not knowing," her father said on a low growl. "I need to know you'll be safe."

"Daddy, from what I've heard you've been through a lot, too. Your chief of staff, Carly Jones, was a murderer who let a man go to prison for her crimes…and for a while it seemed that scandal was all tied up with this one. She tried to kill Selena—because Selena was getting too close trying to prove my innocence when no one else cared—just to hide what she'd done. You can't risk much more, and I won't let you. Just tell the press I'm resting in an undisclosed location until the real killer can be brought to justice. I won't skip out anymore, no matter what."

Her father looked nonplussed. "I can handle scandal, Erin."

"She's right, sir," Chase said. "We don't need a trial by media and we don't need any vigilantes. Word will get out that someone broke in to your house, and we might get even more press out here, not to mention curious bystanders who'd love nothing more than to be heroic on their own. We need to keep Erin safe and out of sight until we have a solid case against Jeffries."

Her father stood silent for a moment and finally nodded and glanced around. "Honey, you witnessed a murder. I just worry—"

"I've survived this long, Daddy. Let Chase do his job. I'll be okay, I promise."

"You can't promise that," her father retorted, pain moving through his eyes.

Erin hugged him, knowing he was remembering her mother. "I'll do my best and...so will Chase."

"I'm counting on that," her father said. Then he shot Chase an unrelenting stare. "You hear me, son?"

"Yes, sir." Chase turned as Captain McCord entered the front door. "I'm going to clear the way right now." He glanced back to Erin and her father. "And Senator, I could use your backup on this decision."

Her father nodded, a grudging admiration flickering through his concern. "I'll make sure of it."

"Don't make me regret this, Zachary."

Chase took in Captain McCord's scowl and the gruff command. The Eagleton estate had settled down now that most of the law-enforcement officers who'd arrived on the scene had gone back to their offices in town.

"I don't plan on it, sir." He took off his black cap and slapped it against his leg. "Look, I had a relationship with Erin in high school, but we're both adults now and...that's over. I can do my job and I'd like to stay on her protection detail."

He wanted to add that he'd done his job both by bringing in Erin Eagleton and by alerting the proper authorities tonight. He'd just have to prove he could handle guarding Erin while he guarded his heart.

"Right." The captain didn't look so sure. "General Meyer believes you *will* do your job, and I'm counting on you. If you need backup or you get in too deep, you'd better come to me, understood?"

"Understood."

Chase turned to check for Erin. She was upstairs

with Brooke Clark, a member of the K-9 team, and her golden retriever, Mercy, packing a few clothes for the trip across the countryside to another location. Brooke would drive ahead of them to the safe house. They'd have to get past the press crowding around the gate, but the local police and some DC police officers would handle that. Erin would be in disguise to protect her identity and to keep anyone from following them.

Chase and Officer Nicholas Cole had a plan to get Erin out and then switch cars midtrip to throw the press, or anyone else watching, off their trail. Nicholas was a former navy SEAL, so he could do this in his sleep. Chase was glad he had Nicholas on his side since Nicholas was engaged to Erin's cousin, Selena. Since Nicholas and Selena had fallen for each other, they'd continued to find proof of Erin's innocence.

Chase planned to turn that up a notch. Nothing had panned out with any of Michael's friends. None of them had known about Michael's discovery of a young relative living in the All Our Kids foster home. Either Michael hadn't confided in anyone but Erin, or the rest of his friends just didn't want to talk about it with a law officer for fear of being in danger. Sometimes the Washington elite made things hard for mere commoners.

He needed to ditch the attitude and concentrate on this case. His wariness toward Erin and her father had become tempered now that he was back near her again. And so should his memories of loving Erin for so long. He had to put the way she looked, the way she smiled, how she seemed so broken and alone, out of his mind. For now. Maybe forever.

He headed to the foot of the stairs to wait for Erin, but he stopped in the big foyer to check his phone messages. A few from work, one from his mom checking on him and…one from Cassie Danvers.

Chase listened to Cassie's message as he watched Erin and Brooke coming down the curving staircase, Mercy leading the way. "Hi, Chase. It's Cassie Danvers. One of my workers remembered something about seeing Michael the day before he died. You might want to hear this."

Chase glanced at his recent calls. The call had come in around 9:00 p.m. He'd call Cassie first thing in the morning.

And he prayed she had information that could help prove Erin's side of the story.

Erin didn't know what to expect when they arrived at the safe house. But the small out-of-the-way town house looked like just about every other house in the neighborhood. Two-story and brick, with a small front yard.

"We're here," Chase said over his shoulder. He'd placed her in the backseat to avoid anyone seeing her.

Erin glanced up at the modest house. From what she could see from the porch light shining through the trees, it was trimmed in white with dark shutters around the windows. The small yard looked neat and manicured and the raised porch held hanging baskets and ferns in pretty stands. A facade.

Seeing this quiet, unassuming home caused something to tug at Erin's heart. She'd lived in a high-rise postage stamp–size apartment near the Potomac River. What would it be like to have a nice house on a quiet street, a house with a pretty backyard and flowers growing in big pots? Flowers she could plant herself, a house she could love and decorate and raise a family in? A house with a husband and a dog to keep her company at night?

Chase opened the door and their eyes met. Erin wondered if he could see the longing in her gaze, but she managed to pull a blank face before he reacted. No need to go there. Her future was shaky at best. Chase couldn't be a part of it, no matter the outcome of this mess. He'd told her once long ago that he didn't think they could make it, that he couldn't live in her world and he didn't expect her to live in his. End of story.

"Ready?" he asked, his gaze sweeping over her like a beam of light.

Unable to speak at first, she nodded. "I hope I'm doing the right thing coming here."

"You should be safe here for a while," he said. "We have several places all over the area and we move people from place to place as needed."

"But you think this will last longer than a while, right?"

"I can't say."

No one could say, so Erin left it at that. Chase helped her out, then went around and let out Valor. A second later, another vehicle showed up and Nicholas Cole and his Rottweiler, Max, came around to join them.

"All clear?" Chase asked, his hand guiding Erin toward the house.

"Clear," Nicholas retorted. "No one followed us."

Erin had learned enough in the past few days to understand members of the K-9 team had their own stoic language. When they didn't want to talk, they didn't. They communicated only the necessary details with no fanfare.

A sharp contrast to the always-talking heads along

the Beltway, but this team sure gave her a sense of security. Chase gave her a sense of security just by looking at her. But those intense glances also gave her a shivering sense of need.

She needed him to understand so many things.

She needed him to forgive her.

She needed him, period.

They hurried her onto the porch and Nicholas used his phone to alert Brooke Clark that they had arrived. The spunky K-9 officer was good at calming scared witnesses and good at protecting them, too. Then Nicholas backed away and stood guard with Max while Chase ushered Erin through the door.

Brooke greeted her with a curt nod. "Hello, Erin. How're ya holding up?"

Erin held her own in spite of rocking on her feet. "I'm fine. Just…tired."

Brooke went into action. "Well, I'm here for as long as you need me. I'll make you a sandwich or get you something to drink."

"That's not necessary," Erin said, worried that she'd already become a problem. "I'm sure you have more important things to do than wait on me."

"I'm planning my wedding," Brooke replied. "While we're here confined together, maybe you can help me with that. You seem to have a great sense of style."

Again that sharp pang of regret mixed with envy, but Erin pushed it away. Chase was right. A lot of wedding plans going on around here, in spite of the gravity of their work.

"I think I can help with that," she said as she mustered up an encouraging smile.

Brooke gave Chase and Nicholas her own encouraging smile. "Good, but first let's get you settled in. There are two bedrooms and a bath upstairs. I'm putting you in the bedroom on the right, close to the guest bathroom. And…we have a security light that shines on that corner of the house. A motion-detection light." To assure Erin, she added, "We also have a good security system."

The unspoken threat of danger hung in the air, but Erin ignored it. She was so tired she could hardly blink, let alone think about someone coming for her again.

"That sounds perfect," she said on a weak croak.

Chase went ahead of her up the stairs. "I'll show you the way."

Erin knew what he was doing. He was allowing Valor to sniff things out. Because no matter where they hid her and no matter how many people they put on her protection detail, Congressman Jeffries wouldn't stop until he found her. The man truly thought he could still wiggle his way out of murdering the mother of his little boy and his son Michael.

For a moment, she considered leaving again. She needed to run so no one else would get hurt or possibly die because of her. But common sense stopped her. If she ran, all of these people would have worked in vain. She had to stay and somehow find proof of her innocence.

EIGHT

Brooke showed Erin the bathroom. "It's stocked with fresh towels and toiletries. Sleep as late as you'd like. No pressure here."

"Thank you," Erin said when they'd reached the bedroom. A lamp on a bedside table brightened the room.

Erin glanced up at Chase, but he only gave her a grim nod and said, "Looks good. I need to talk to Nicholas and then I'll come back and check on you."

"No need," she told him, wondering why he seemed so tense. But then, why wouldn't he seem that way? He'd gone out on a limb for her since she'd returned, so he might regret that already. Probably regretted ever getting involved with her again.

But he searched for you...for five months. He found you in spite of the odds and he's been fighting for you. Chase was putting his life on the line for her. He'd always fought for what was right. Maybe that's why he'd walked away from her.

He'd believed he was doing what was right for her.

Erin wanted to tell him how much she appreciated him, but Chase didn't give her a chance. "Okay, then. See you in the morning."

He whirled, ordered Valor out, and they stomped down the stairs.

After Chase left, Brooke's eyebrows shot up. "He sure is focused on protecting you."

"He's focused on getting to the bottom of things," Erin corrected. "I'm not sure he fully trusts that I'm telling the truth."

Brooke turned at the door. "Oh, and I think you're wrong about Chase. From what I can tell, he's very concerned about keeping you safe. Which is probably why he and Nicholas will be patrolling the front yard for the rest of the night."

Erin woke to the smells of coffee and bacon, and the light of a bright sunbeam slicing through the closed wooden blinds. Glancing at the ornate little clock on the bedside table, she saw that it was past nine. Somehow, she'd managed to fall into a deep sleep.

Voices downstairs brought her up out of the bed. Grabbing some of the clothes she'd packed last night, she hurried to the bathroom and freshened up. Wearing a button-up cotton shirt and jeans with sandals, she shook out her hair and opened the bedroom door.

Valor lay in front of the door. The dog glanced up at her and woofed a greeting. She heard a "Come" command from downstairs, and Valor stood and hurried ahead of her.

Surprised, Erin had to smile. Valor was her protector, too. But like Chase, the faithful dog was trained to protect her. She couldn't get attached to either of them.

She moved down the stairs and steeled herself for seeing Chase again in the light of day. He and Nicholas sat at the kitchen table, nursing big mugs of steaming coffee. Brooke moved between the stove and the table with a plate of toast and a bowl of scrambled eggs. A plate of bacon was already on the table.

Chase stood and gave Erin an appreciative appraisal, but his expression stayed close to stern, the half smile tight with unspoken tension.

"Good morning," Brooke said. She went about her business as if it were a perfectly natural thing to be here with two other K-9 officers and their furry partners, along with a "person of interest" in a scandalous murder case.

"Hi." Erin felt as if she'd walked in on something. "You didn't have to cook for me, Brooke."

"I didn't," Brooke said. "They cooked. I'm just serving it up."

Nicholas sat up and then politely stood at the sight of her. Chase shot her a probing glance then sent what looked like a warning to Nicholas. Had something else happened last night?

"What's wrong?" she asked. Brooke handed her a cup of coffee and Erin gladly took it.

"Nothing," Chase said, moving to help her with a chair. "How'd you sleep?"

"Fine." She sank down, her gaze moving from him to Nicholas. The tall blond with the golden-brown eyes nodded curtly but didn't give anything away.

"Chase, is something going on, something I need to know about?" she asked, her hand curling around the warmth of the coffee mug.

"Nothing for you to be concerned about," he said. "We had a quiet night." He leaned up and grabbed a piece of toast. "I need to…visit some people…regarding the case."

"Who?"

"I can't tell you who," he said. "Just wanted you to be aware that I won't be able to hang around much today."

Well, he did have a good excuse to give her the brush-off. "I don't expect you to hang around."

"She'll be fine with us," Brooke interrupted. "Right, Nicholas?"

"I'll be here," he said, his tone as calm as the blue sky outside, his demeanor steady and secure. Did Nicholas resent her because Selena had been put in danger a couple of months ago, too?

"Why can't you tell me anything?" Erin asked Chase, needing to know if he trusted her yet. "Since I'm at the center of this investigation, I think I have a right to know."

Chase put down his half-eaten toast. "Look, Erin, we've got a lot of angles to cover on this case and I'm not at liberty to keep you posted on what I'm doing. I have my orders and—"

"And babysitting me isn't a high priority. I get that and I understand why you brought in Nicholas for backup. And maybe even that's why you brought in Brooke, so I wouldn't feel so isolated. But if this involves me, I'd like to hear it."

"It doesn't," Chase replied. "Just routine questioning. I'm trying to establish a few things—timelines, people who talked to Michael—"

"You mean, people who talked to him besides me? Are you trying to prove I'm right or show that I'm wrong?"

"He believes you're right," Brooke said. "We all do." She took a sip of her coffee. "But he has to do his job, Erin."

Erin realized she'd raised her voice, and she immediately regretted her tone, given how they'd all helped her. "Okay. Sorry."

She didn't press Chase anymore. But she didn't have an appetite either. So she grabbed a piece of dry toast and mumbled "Excuse me," then took her coffee to the front of the house.

Standing at the window, she stared out at the deserted street and tried to center herself in prayers. Until a hand on her arm pulled her around.

"Don't stand by the window," Chase said, taking her coffee out of her hand and carefully placing it on a nearby table. "Erin, I'm sorry. I have to follow a few leads I've been working on and I didn't want to worry you with details that might not pan out."

"Okay." She wanted to believe he was doing this for her, but she still worried that history would repeat itself. Would he walk away because he still didn't believe *in* her?

"Erin, I need you to understand—"

"That you're just doing your job. Got it." She shut her eyes for a moment. "I wish this could be over."

"It will be. We're all working toward finding the truth." He touched her, lifting her chin with the pad of his thumb. The tenderness in that act made her want to crumble against him and absorb some of that quiet strength. "Hey, we all believe you and we're getting closer to the real story every day. Your life has been threatened several times over."

"It's hard to let go of…running," she admitted. "I let everyone down. My father. Michael. You."

"You don't owe me anything," he replied, his tone

quiet, his eyes full of regret. "I mean, who knew we'd wind up together again, like this?"

Erin regretted acting like a spoiled brat. "I'm sorry. I'm still reeling from everything that's happened over the last few months." Tears she'd tried to hold back spilled down her face. "I haven't even had time to grieve Michael's death. I feel horrible that I wanted to end things with him, that I couldn't…love him enough. But I never dreamed that the last time I saw him would turn out to be our last time together. That he'd be dead before that day ended."

Chase gave her an understanding stare and dropped his hand away. "It must have been hard, watching him die that way."

"Yes. Awful. I begged the congressman to help him, to call 911, to do something." She stopped, grasping at a memory. "He called Leon Ridge instead of 911."

Chase's expression darkened. "So Ridge wasn't already on the estate?"

"No. I was holding Michael's head on my lap and… I placed my jacket over him, trying to stop the bleeding." She pushed at her hair, memories hitting her full force. "I remember glancing up at the congressman and when I saw him on the phone, I thought he was getting help. But…I think he pretended to be doing that because instead of giving our location, he barked an order. 'Do it now,' he said. Then he hung up and that's when he pulled the gun on me."

Chase jotted notes in his pocket notebook. "We're searching his phone records to check on who he called. We checked Michael's records, but we didn't check the congressman's records since he insisted Michael was the target, or so we thought. A 911 call came in later, so what you say makes sense. If he called Leon Ridge that means Ridge not only helped the congressman try to hide what he'd done, but your testimony with a phone record to back it up can help prove Ridge was there at the same time you were."

"He showed up right after that call so he had to have been nearby," Erin said. "Michael...wasn't responding. I couldn't get him to wake up."

"I'm sorry you had to go through that."

They stood there, inches apart. Chase reached out his hand toward her again and then dropped it. "I'd better get going. McCord needs to hear this, and I'll get the crime-scene techs' help with going back over the time-line and the evidence we have so far."

"Of course. You need to do whatever it takes to prove that Congressman Jeffries isn't the man everyone thinks he is."

"I'm working on it," he said. Then he did reach over to touch her face one more time, his fingers brushing at her tears. "I failed you once, Erin. I won't do that again, I promise." With a muffled sigh, he tugged her close, his fingers tangling in her hair. "I just need you to keep the faith, okay?"

She nodded and pulled away, too shocked and emotional to be coherent. She couldn't depend on anyone right now, not even Chase. But she wanted to trust him, so she agreed with him. "Okay." Then she crossed her arms against her stomach to keep from rushing into his arms. "Chase, be careful."

He winked at her. "Always."

She watched as he loaded up Valor and headed out for the day. When she turned around, Brooke was perched against the wall across from the kitchen.

"You and Chase…sure have a history."

Erin let out a gulp of a chuckle. "Yeah, you could say that." Embarrassed, she brushed at her tears.

Brooke lifted off the doorjamb and came to stand in front of Erin. "I think you two definitely have some unfinished business."

"I hope you don't mind interviewing Virginia here in the kitchen," Cassie Danvers said to Chase later that afternoon. She slapped peanut butter and jelly onto thick slices of bread and then threw them together before she moved on and stirred some sort of fruity drink into a giant pitcher, all without batting an eye at the constant interruptions from several kids of various ages. "It's almost lunchtime so we have to stay on top of things."

"I don't mind at all," Chase said, glancing at his watch. He'd stationed Valor out on the porch with a command to stay. Had over three hours passed since he'd left Erin back at the safe house?

"In a hurry, Officer Zachary?" Cassie asked, giving him a firm smile.

"No, no. Just wondering where my morning went," he admitted. "I've been filing reports and fielding questions all morning. Not to mention, trying to track down people who might be able to shed some light on this case."

"You don't look too pleased."

"I haven't found anything substantial," he replied, fatigue tugging at him like a wet fog. He was waiting to hear back about Congressman Jeffries's phone records, too. Everyone had been focusing on Erin's missing phone and Michael's records up until now.

Cassie dried her hands on a dish towel and came over

to him with a fresh cup of coffee. "On the house," she said on a droll note. Then she got herself a cup. "Sorry you have to wait a few more minutes for Virginia. It's been a busy morning around here."

Chase could see why Captain McCord had fallen hard for Cassie. The two had met when an intruder had tried to set the foster home on fire, and McCord and his K-9 partner, Glory, had tracked a kid's blue glove back to the house. One of the kids, whom they had now identified as Tommy Benson, had sneaked out that night and he'd seen the congressman holding a gun. Apparently, someone had spotted the kid there and decided to torch the foster home to make sure none of the kids talked. Which was why they were all still here in a safe house until this case was wrapped up.

Chase got sick to his stomach, thinking how any man would deliberately set fire to a foster home to hide his crimes. Especially if that man had actually started the home and had remained its champion throughout the years.

At least something good had come out of that horror.

After the captain and Cassie had been around each other through attacks and near-death experiences, they had bonded and fallen in love. Cassie was down-to-earth and smart, not to mention kind of pretty with all that red hair and those flashing green eyes. She'd been a rock throughout the past few months. Chase figured it'd take a certain kind of woman to measure up to his formidable captain. This one obviously did.

"You've had to deal with a lot lately," he said, taking the coffee with gratitude. "I guess you'll be glad to get back to normal one day."

"I gave up on normal a long time ago," she replied.

A ball rolled by and she stuck out her foot to stop it. "Hey, not in the kitchen, remember?"

A young boy gave her a sheepish grin then grabbed the ball and darted to the other room.

"Summertime," she said to Chase. "I will be so glad when we're back at a place we can call our own, hopefully before school starts up." Her smile radiated strength. "If Gavin has his way, that could happen sooner than later." Then she put a finger to her lips. "But I can't talk about that right now."

Chase lifted one eyebrow. "Oh, okay." Then he held up his hands, palms out. "Captain doesn't talk about anything much anyway."

"He is the strong, silent type," she quipped, clearly in love.

"I hear that." Chase wanted to find some peace with this case, too. And he kind of wished he could find someone to share his life with. Erin came to mind, but his feelings for her were as scattered as the old oaks sprinkled across the countryside.

He blinked and refocused. "Now…what do you think Virginia needs to tell me?"

Cassie glanced around to make sure they were alone. "Virginia will be in soon. She's on the phone talking to Lana Gomez, checking up on little Juan."

Juan Gomez. The little boy at the center of this mystery and the young son of Congressman Jeffries. His mother had been tossed away like a bag of garbage, killed for having an affair with the wrong man.

"How's he doing?"

"He's great. Lana loves him and well…she and Adam are engaged and talking marriage. That kind of thing seems to be in the air these days."

Chase grinned at her smile. "So I hear." He grinned, then thought about how he'd touched Erin's face this morning and remembered how much he'd wanted to kiss her. But all of those feelings he'd tried so hard to bury would have to wait.

He wouldn't make a move toward getting Erin back until he had Harland Jeffries behind bars.

NINE

A slender woman with brown hair and matching eyes hurried into the kitchen and let out a breathless sigh. "I'm so sorry. Got carried away talking about Juan. I miss that little boy so much."

Chase stood and shook her hand. "Thanks for agreeing to meet with me, Ms. Johnson. I won't keep you long."

Virginia sank down with a look of fear mixed with duty, kind of as if she might be facing a firing squad. "I wish I'd remembered this earlier, but it's been completely crazy these last few months."

"It's okay," Chase said, hoping to reassure her. "You've all been under a lot of pressure. I'm glad you remembered it now. So…what *do* you remember? Did Michael Jeffries come by here at any time during the week he died?"

Virginia bobbed her head, her eyes widening. "Yes, he sure did. It was earlier on that day—the day he died."

She averted her eyes, but Cassie gave her what looked like an encouraging glance. "Virginia, just tell the truth."

"I was trying to calm Juan. He had just come to

us that day and we were all concerned since he was so young and alone. I was nervous and I guess Juan was sensing that. Mr. Jeffries stormed in the door and stood there, staring at Juan and me." She glanced over at Cassie. "Cassie had taken one of the kids for a checkup so I was there alone with some of the younger kids."

"Did he say anything about why he was at the foster home?" Chase asked.

"No. It was the strangest thing. He made small talk and said he was just stopping by to check on us and see if we needed anything and then he asked me about Juan. Where did he come from? Did I know his parents? I told him Juan's mother had died in a terrible accident." She shrugged. "We had just heard about his mother's death and we didn't know at the time that she'd been…murdered. I was still sad about that so I didn't say much more."

"What happened next?"

"He came toward Juan and asked if he could hold him."

"Did you let him take the boy?"

"No. I'd changed Juan and he only had on a diaper. I wanted to get him into some clean clothes first." She shook her head, her hair flying out around her face in brown ribbons. "Two of the kids started fighting so I took Juan with me into the kitchen. When I came back to the living room, Mr. Jeffries was gone."

Cassie leaned forward. "She got on with her day and then later everything changed. We got attacked and… we had to move."

"I know I should have remembered earlier but…I was so scared when all of this happened I never connected on that moment until Cassie asked if I remembered Michael ever coming by here right before he died." She shrugged. "He and the congressman both came by a lot anyway since we were so close to Congressman Jeffries's estate. They were around so much, I never thought about that day."

"Understandable under the circumstances," Chase replied, thinking Virginia could be attractive if she wasn't so uptight. But she seemed like a nice lady and nothing about her indicated that she was lying. Virginia Johnson probably didn't know how to lie anyway. She definitely cared about these kids.

Chase thanked the two women and headed back toward DC, his thoughts swirling. It wasn't much, but it did prove that Michael had been upset about something and that he'd come to verify Juan's being at the foster home. Had he seen the birthmark on little Juan that matched his own and his father's? If he had gone to confront his father about this the night he died, Erin had to be telling the truth about walking up on their altercation.

But what if Michael had confided in her at dinner? She and Michael could have argued. They'd been seen leaving the restaurant around nine, and the stamp on the restaurant receipt verified that. Chase had seen Erin at the National Monument around 10:00 p.m. The call to report the murder had come in around 11:30 p.m.

Had Erin gone to see Michael again that night after she'd stopped to talk to Chase? She'd told them over and over that she'd arrived at the estate a little before eleven and witnessed the congressman and Michael struggling. Then the gun went off and Michael fell to the ground. After she and the congressman had argued, he'd threatened her, held the gun on her. He'd called for help and

Leon Ridge had shown up, and after shooting the congressman, he'd put her in his car around eleven twenty. She remembered that from the clock on the car's dash.

The congressman had waited for them to leave, but according to his own statement he'd passed out briefly before he'd called for help. He could have died and everyone would have assumed Erin had killed both of them.

But they still needed to find her car and they needed to find the murder weapon. Some of the team members were on that right now, along with the FBI and the Metro Police. Leon Ridge could make things a whole lot easier if he'd just give them the rest of the story. Fat chance on that one, especially if he was being coerced to take the rap.

Deciding to check in with the forensic team, Chase dialed up Fiona Fargo, the technician dynamo who helped the whole team. She'd know if the techs who'd been going back over Ridge's car had found anything. And she'd tell Chase what she knew since Fiona was a romantic at heart. Fiona had her own thing going with fellow officer Chris Torrence. She wanted Erin to be exonerated and she wanted Erin and Chase to find each other again.

Fat chance on that one, too.

"Hey, I was just about to call you," Fiona said without preamble.

Chase held his breath. "Tell me something good, please."

"Good and better," Fiona replied in what sounded like a happy tone. "They found strands of honey-blond hair in Leon Ridge's car. In the front passenger seat."

"And?"

"They're a positive match for Erin's DNA."

"Okay, but that doesn't show she was forced into the car."

"Does blood on the door handle count then?"

"Yes, yes, it does, but whose blood?"

"They found two different types of blood," Fiona said. "One is a match for Erin—just a smidgen on a door handle. But we also found a print on the door handle, kind of out of sight. The fingerprint belongs to Erin. But the rest of the blood belongs to Michael Jeffries."

Chase let out a whoop. "That matches what Erin told me this morning. She said she tried to stop Michael's bleeding with her jacket. She must have had his blood all over her clothes and hands." But he wondered about finding *her* blood. "Maybe she injured herself since she was forced inside the car."

"Makes sense to me," Fiona replied.

Chase asked her about the congressman making a call to Leon. "Find out who he called for me, okay?"

"We're on it," Fiona replied. "We're gonna get this thing figured out, Chase."

Chase hoped she was right. "Great. Anything else to make me smile?"

"Nope. But as soon as we search those particular phone records, I might have more. We've already pulled his records regarding the corruption charges, of course. We might find something there to link to the night of the murder, too."

"Keep me posted," Chase replied. "I'm heading back to check Erin and to relieve Brooke and Nicholas."

"I have one more thing," Fiona said.

"I'm listening."

"The techs did a really thorough search of the car

and they found an old photo pushed up underneath one of the floor mats."

"A photo of what?"

"Not what, but who," Fiona replied. "The image looks a lot like Rosa Gomez."

"Really?" Chase's pulse jumped. "Maybe we need to ask Leon why that photo was in his car."

"Yeah, I think that's a good idea," Fiona replied.

"Okay. Thanks, Fiona."

Chase ended the call and let out a sigh of relief. Now they were getting down to the details. Important details.

He needed more than his gut instincts and a sketchy account from a paid henchman to prove that Erin didn't have anything to do with Michael's death. Captain Mc-Cord and General Meyer could allow for only so much before they started buckling down on him to end this thing.

Chase wanted nothing more. But he wanted to end it with the truth and he wanted to prove Erin's innocence and catch Congressman Jeffries and get his confession, too. If they could get the truth out of Leon Ridge, they'd be halfway there.

But he needed to find Congressman Jeffries, and soon. A man like him would become desperate when his carefully controlled house of cards came tumbling down. And that scared Chase.

By the time he arrived back at the safe house, Chase was tired but hopeful. Valor looked bored. He liked doing his job, not traipsing around with his partner. Chase had taken a few minutes at the foster home to show the kids some of Valor's best moves. A good workout, but no real action. A good night's sleep would be nice for both of them, however. Chase knew a lot of action could be around the corner.

Three days later, Erin had read two books, flipped through several bride magazines and made notes to help Brooke and Selena and whatever other bride might come along. And she'd cooked twice, a Mexican casserole for dinner last night and a chocolate cake for the guards who'd been watching over her day and night.

So far, the days had become almost mundane and ordinary, except for officers and K-9 partners moving around the perimeters of the house and yard. For the hundredth time, she checked the clock and wondered where Chase was. This had become her routine.

Brooke and her partner, Mercy, kept Erin company during the day. Or rather, stood watch over her, to protect her and to keep her contained, Erin had decided. But she didn't mind having Brooke and the lovable Mercy with her. They talked about weddings and marriage, and then compared other girlie things. Brooke was dedicated to her job and now, to a veterinarian named Jonas Parker and his son, Felix. Another happy ending that only left Erin sad and confused.

"I don't think I'll ever get married," she'd said this afternoon after they watched a romantic comedy. "Men are too hard to figure out."

Brooke laughed at that comment. "I so agree. But you know they can be worth the trouble. And besides, figuring them out is part of the fun."

"Hmm. I suppose you're right."

"Chase has done some fancy footwork on your behalf," Brooke reminded her. "We're slowly gathering evidence to prove you did witness the death of Michael Jeffries—not commit it."

Erin was thankful for that, at least. "He told me about the hair follicles inside Leon Ridge's car. My hair." She told Brooke how the hit man had grabbed her by the hair and shoved her onto the front seat. "I really thought he'd shoot me and toss me out the door."

"And they found traces of your blood," Brooke said, shaking her head.

"I skinned my knuckles," Erin replied, remembering how excited Chase had been on Monday when he'd asked her about that. Chase had been careful in what he could say, so she suspected he knew much more than he'd told her. But Leon Ridge refused to confess to anything other than what he kept repeating—that the congressman had accidentally shot his son and then he'd panicked and called Leon for help. True enough, if you didn't consider that Erin had witnessed the whole thing and that she wasn't supposed to be alive to tell the truth.

"He's running scared," Chase had explained about Leon. "He knows he'll be next if he squeals the rest. You're a solid eyewitness, so Leon would rather take the fall than admit that."

"Good thing you did skin your hand," Brooke said over lunch. "It supports your statement. Ridge forced you into that car and sooner or later, he'll have to tell us why he did that."

Slowly, one by one, the Capitol K-9 team members were beginning to see that Erin had been telling the truth from the beginning.

She had to wonder still if Chase truly believed her. He'd been in and out, taking turns with Nicholas and

Brooke, and several other team members to make sure she stayed alive.

Was he avoiding her now that he had her safely tucked away?

When she heard his truck pull up, she let out the breath she'd been holding. He was safe for now. Chase was working day and night to help her, so he couldn't doubt her. She sent up a prayer of thanks for everything he'd done for her, but Erin was beginning to depend on him way too much.

What would happen once this case was solved, once they caught the people responsible? Would Chase walk away again? Would he forget all about her? He loved his job and he had built a good life without her. Why should that change once this was over?

She wouldn't think about that right now. Knowing she couldn't hide out here forever, she asked God to protect those who worked to protect her. What else could she do right now?

Trust in God, she reminded herself again.

For a few hours, she'd have Chase mostly to herself. For now at least, he was home. Home, where they could be together for what was becoming very precious time.

TEN

Home. In spite of the constant watchfulness of several interagency law-enforcement teams guarding her around the clock, Chase figured Erin was probably ready to go home. But when he walked in and saw her each day, she did look healthier and happier than when he'd found her in those dark woods. Having this quiet reprieve had helped her a lot, but with Captain Mc-Cord and General Meyer demanding daily reports and reminding him that she was technically still under suspicion, Chase had tried to stay on the job so he could prove them wrong. Which meant he hadn't been able to spend as much time with Erin as he would have liked.

"I think Selena wants Erin to be in our wedding," Nicholas had told him earlier. "So we need to keep at it and get this case over with and done. She won't plan our wedding if Erin can't be her bridesmaid."

Chase agreed with that notion. But with Leon Ridge refusing to talk in spite of the evidence mounting against him, Chase was beginning to feel hopeless again. No one had seen hide nor hair of Congressman Jeffries either.

"He's out there," Captain McCord said at an early

morning briefing. They'd watched his estate and his apartment near the Capitol building, but both remained closed up and vacant. "We've had leads that place him in New York, Costa Rica and even Europe, but none of them have panned out. I want him brought in as much as the rest of you do."

Chase wanted that, too. The congressman probably *was* down in the Caymans or somewhere in Europe by now. But Chase also wanted to spend time with Erin, time that didn't require a constant watch and the tension of knowing someone wanted her dead. He valued the precious moments they'd spent together over the past few days, but he could tell she wanted to go back to her apartment in the city, back to her life before…

Before Michael's death?

Or way back to the day she'd told Chase she was going on that summer safari with several of her rich friends? A trip her father had given her for graduation and had insisted she needed to take…to expand her horizons. The final straw for Chase since she'd been willing to go and leave him behind.

They'd broken up that day, but Erin had tried to reach out to him, hoping Chase would forgive her, when she returned a few weeks later. But…he'd left early for college and…he refused to return her calls after that. Didn't see the point. They weren't meant to be together anyway.

Who was the stupid one now?

Who would have believed all these years later they'd be tossed back together in such a strange way? Or that his feelings for her would come back so sure and strong?

Trying to see this time of forced confinement as a blessing, Chase wondered how Erin felt about him. Did she still care? They talked late into the night, sitting together on the couch until she got sleepy. Then she'd go upstairs and he'd stay there with Valor, guarding the house and getting very little sleep since his mind was all wrapped up in this investigation. He didn't care about sleep right now. He cared only about Erin. He cared only about keeping her alive.

Maybe…after this was over, they could have a second chance with each other. He'd changed and so had she. Surely with prayer and hope and a new maturity, they could start fresh.

She only wanted a do-over, a second chance with Chase.

In spite of the circumstances, Erin loved waiting for him to come here each night. It almost felt like normal life. Almost.

When he came in the door today, Valor on his heels, Erin glanced up from her perch at the kitchen table, her gaze meeting his. "Hi," she said, relief sweeping over her. She worried about him when he was out there working.

Chase nodded, a half smile playing across his lips while he assessed the room and her. Valor gave Chase an expectant glance.

"Go on. Tell Erin hello," Chase said. She loved how this had become an endearing part of their routine.

Valor trotted over to Erin and she went down on her knees to give the big dog a pat and a hug. Even though Valor still had on his protective Kevlar vest, Erin managed to snuggle against him. "Hello, my sweet boy. How you doing?"

Valor's dog smile widened. The big dog glanced back at Chase as if to show his partner he was Erin's favorite.

Chase cleared his throat. "We're both fine, thank you."

Erin lifted her eyes to stare at him and saw the need in his eyes, the same need that caught hold of her each time she was around him. "How…how was your day?"

It *was* a normal question, asked on a normal summer day with the sun shining outside and the smell of dinner wafting from the stove. But the hope tearing at her heart was anything but normal. Her longing had changed from wishing she could prove her innocence to wishing she could make Chase love her again.

That was a wish that might not come true, a future that couldn't be seen, but a longing that couldn't be denied.

Trust in the Lord. Have faith. Do not despair.

The words from Psalms came to her in a rush of awareness.

Chase must have seen the calamity forming in her eyes. He reached down and pulled her up, his gaze holding hers, his silence speaking more than words ever could.

"Erin—"

"I'm back," Brooke called as she opened the laundry room door and came into the kitchen. "Bath towels are all folded." Taking one look at them, she stopped, her mouth falling open in surprise, and then turned and headed the other way. "And now I'm going to check on the cleaning supplies."

Erin smiled at Chase and then started giggling. "I've never seen her so embarrassed before."

He chuckled back, looking relaxed for the first time

in days. "Her timing stinks, but dinner does smell good."

Enjoying the moment, Erin said, "And what would have happened if Brooke hadn't interrupted us?"

"This," he said, lowering his head to hers.

Erin waited for his kiss, waited for his touch, waited for what seemed like a lifetime to see forgiveness in his eyes.

And then the air was pierced with a boom and she heard barking outside and boots hitting the hardwood floors.

In the next moment, she found herself down on the floor with Chase covering her and Valor dancing in an angry circle, his barks matching the woofs coming from another officer's dog.

Brooke came charging in from the laundry room, Mercy on her heels. "Someone's shooting at us."

Chase went into action, leaving Valor with Erin. He radioed Dylan Ralsey, the team member who'd relieved Nicholas today. Dylan and his partner, Tico, were out front.

"I'm on it," Dylan replied. "Not sure where that shot came from."

"I'll check the back," Chase reported in response. He motioned to where Brooke crouched by the back door of the kitchen. "Keep her here, okay?"

She bobbed her head and crawled toward Erin and Chase. Chase turned and checked on Erin. "You okay?"

"I think so. I'm sorry they keep coming after me."

"We'll talk about sorry later," he said. "Right now, I need to get out there."

"Be careful."

Chase rushed to the back door, gun lifted, and opened it before he crouched low and sent Valor out.

Brooke slid to the door and locked it. Then she rushed back to the safety of the cabinets across from the other counter. She held her revolver in the air.

Erin glanced at the weapon and then back at Brooke. "What do you want me to do?"

"Don't get shot," Brooke said on a reasonable note.

Erin let out a breath. "Agreed. I need something—" She spotted a rolling pin and reached up onto the counter and grabbed it. Not exactly a gun, but a weapon she could hurl at someone or use to trip them up.

Another shot pierced the dusk and shattered a nearby window, the echo reverberating out over the neighborhood. Then every dog along the street joined in the barking.

Erin lifted herself up to sit against the kitchen cabinets. "Are you all right?" she asked Brooke.

"Fine," Brooke said on a winded breath, her gun held with both hands now. "I'm kind of used to this." She checked her weapon. "Someone wants to shut you up permanently."

"It's him," Erin said on a hiss. "Congressman Jeffries won't stop until I'm dead. I'm the only witness to what really happened that night, and if he can't frame me for Michael's murder, he'll make sure I never talk to anyone again."

"We lost the scent," Chase said thirty minutes later to Dylan. Same song, second verse. Or maybe the third or fourth verse. Someone had managed to trace them again, but how? "I'm thinking they've planted a GPS or bug on one of our vehicles or maybe somewhere on

Erin's clothes." She always wore a dark hoodie, but he couldn't figure how anyone could have planted a tracer on that old thing.

"We need to read in McCord and the general," Dylan said, his weapon lowered while he scanned the street behind the house.

Patrol cars roamed the streets while officers went around the neighborhood on foot to question potential witnesses, but the yards here were wide and spread apart. So far, no one had seen the shooter.

"That'll go over real well," Chase retorted, his cell already out. Then he noticed a car parked haphazardly in a driveway down the street. "Hey, I don't remember seeing that car before."

"Those big hedges blocked our line of sight," Dylan replied, already heading that way. "But you're right. The patrol cars had to have come by here. No reports, so I think this is a new development."

The navy blue sports car looked familiar, but it also looked dirty. Too dirty.

Dylan turned to scan the street. "Maybe a neighbor heard the shots and got out of the vehicle and ran in the house."

"Maybe," Chase said, alerting Valor. "Let's check it out."

Valor started his ground-to-air sniffing again and immediately alerted when they reached the car. The big dog trotted to the open driver's door and stopped to stare. But when he whimpered, Chase got a tingling sensation alone his neck.

"Interesting," Dylan said, his weapon at the ready.

"Yep." Chase held his service revolver out in front of him, but he had a sick feeling that Valor had alerted on this car for a reason. If Chase took a guess, he'd say Valor knew the owner of this car.

He came around the sleek, mud-encased hood, thinking he'd probably find something inside this car to make his day go from bad to worse. "I know this vehicle," he said on a low whisper.

"Oh, yeah?" Dylan walked so silently, Chase turned to find him looking over his shoulder. "*Oh*, yeah," he said again as they both stared into the front passenger's seat.

"This is Erin's car," Chase said, his heart doing a fast drop to his feet. "Valor must have picked up on her scent or maybe the scent of whoever left it here."

"Sure is a mess," Dylan retorted on a dry note. "Almost like it's been hidden in the woods for…say… months."

"Yeah." Chase did a quick scan of the houses lining the street. "I think someone is sending us a message."

"The shooter?"

"Or the congressman who sent the shooter." Chase figured someone had deliberately left the car here. "Maybe the congressman did this." He nudged closer. "Or maybe someone else."

"And the bloody jacket inside?"

"That's Erin's, too," Chase said. "She was wearing that the night I saw her. The night Michael Jeffries died." He did a sweep of the area and then stared back into the car. "Only, Erin left this covering Michael at the scene. Ridge grabbed her and put her in his car, but our techs found Michael's blood in the car. That matches what Erin told me about the jacket."

"Hmm," Dylan said. "Then how did the jacket get in her car?"

"Good question. I'd guess Leon put it there, but… he's in jail."

Quiet. And then Dylan stated the obvious. "So that's not her blood but Michael Jeffries's."

"I think so," Chase replied as he carefully checked the cramped backseat then headed around to the trunk. "Which proves she was definitely there when he got shot. We need to look inside this trunk, too."

Dylan radioed their location then turned back to Chase. "Right, but…let's go back to all the blood on that jacket. What do you think?"

Chase lowered his weapon and turned to face his friend. "I think, just like Erin told me, that that's Michael's blood." Then he pulled out his phone again. "And I think we need to get this vehicle processed as soon as possible. I don't like this." He started back toward the house.

"Hey?"

"Stay here," he said to Dylan. "I have to check on Erin."

"Got it. Make sure she's okay."

"On my way," Chase called, running now with Valor by his side.

He had to get back to Erin, and he prayed he wouldn't be too late.

Mercy growled low.

Erin's cell buzzed, but it was high up on the kitchen counter. Too dangerous to reach right now.

Brooke glanced at Erin and pointed to the front door of the house. Erin held on to the rolling pin then mouthed, "If anyone comes up this hall, I'm going to throw this and then you can—"

"Shoot them," Brooke replied, her calm as clear as the two words she'd just spoken.

Erin felt that same calm. They had Mercy with them and she was so ready to pounce. That lock wouldn't hold if someone wanted in here and…with even the alarm sounding, someone could easily shoot at them and run.

Too late to worry about that now. A *pop, pop* hissed over the house.

Someone had just shot open the front door lock.

ELEVEN

Chase could hear Mercy's frenzied barks now mixing with Valor's. Radioing for backup, he hurried through the backyard and tried the kitchen door. Locked. Because he'd told them to lock it. He headed toward the basement door. It stood open.

When he heard a crashing sound, he moved around to the front of the house only to find the front door wide open.

"Erin?" he called out. "It's me. It's Chase."

Valor's snarls and barks settled to a low growl. "Search." Chase carefully went through the door after the eager dog, noting the lock had been shot off.

"Brooke?"

"We're in here," she called, her voice firm.

Chase hurried to the kitchen and found Erin and Brooke crouched near a counter with Valor now standing guard.

Valor whimpered a greeting and both women jumped up and started talking.

"All right, one at a time," Chase said, lowering his gun. He reached out and grabbed at Erin. "Are you both okay?"

Brooke stood and did a neck roll. "Affirmative. A man dressed in dark clothing with a mask over his face. Mercy scared him off."

"And Brooke shot at him," Erin replied, terror still in her eyes.

"Erin pinged him with a rolling pin. He should have a really big knock on his head."

Amazed, Chase radioed Nicholas that everything was okay, then explained to Brooke that they had a situation.

"What kind of situation?" Erin asked, worry edging her eyes as the whole house became flooded with law-enforcement personnel.

He'd have to tell her sooner or later. Might as well be now. "We found your car."

She let out a gasp. "What? Where?"

"Someone left it down the street," he said. "It had your jacket in it. And Erin, there was blood all over the jacket."

Erin leaned back against a cabinet. "I…I used it to try to stop the bleeding. That's Michael's blood, Chase. Remember I told you?" She put a hand to her mouth, tears misting at her eyes. "Who would leave it here knowing someone would find it?"

"Someone who *wanted* us to find it," he said, pulling her close. "Someone who's running scared."

"And determined to make me look like a murderer," she retorted, turning away to stare out into the growing darkness. "But…this could also prove I'm telling the truth, right?"

"Whoever planted that jacket in your car probably thinks you're either dead right about now since they sent a hit man to kill you or…that you haven't told us everything."

She glanced beyond him. "You mean, they sent the shooter and then they left my car here, thinking I'd be dead, but the evidence would be here for all to see."

Chase's radio buzzed. "We'll talk more later. I have to help process the scene at the car," he said. "And… don't clean up anything. We need to check for prints at the front door, in here and in the basement. Brooke, do a search for any bullet fragments or slugs. You'll both have to give your statements, too."

Brooke started moving around the room, already doing her job.

He motioned to a nearby patrol officer. "Don't leave this room."

The officer nodded, his expression somber.

"I'm taking Valor with me," he said, giving Erin one last glance. "Stay safe."

Erin lifted a hand. "I left that bloody jacket lying by Michael. Leon dragged me away. I didn't take the jacket with me."

Chase came back over to Erin. "We'll get this figured out." Then he gave Erin what he hoped was a reassuring glance. "We're going to stop this, I promise."

She only nodded and then turned away again. When Chase glanced back, he could see the dejection in her body language. She'd folded over into herself as she tried to shut out yet another horrible reminder of that night.

"We need to bring her in," Captain McCord repeated later that night after they'd finished up with the crime scene. "The only place she's going to be safe is in protective custody."

Metro Police detective David Delvecchio grunted and looked bored. "The man's got a point, Zachary. This woman has been hiding out all over the countryside and up until you brought her in, she's been pretty resourceful out there. Now whoever's behind this has upped the ante."

"Erin *is* the ante," Chase said, glancing around the briefing room to see who else wanted to argue with him. "But you're right. She has a better chance of surviving if we move her to a place he can't figure out. I want to take her out away from the city. He somehow finds out where we're keeping her. He knows she's in our custody, but…we're running out of options."

"Then let us protect her," Secret Service agent Dan Calvert said. He'd been involved in this investigation since General Meyer's office and the White House had been breached. "Don't be so stubborn about this. You've tried and…they keep coming."

"And they will find her again," Chase said, afraid to let Erin out of his sight. "Or do you still want her under wraps because she's still high on the list of suspects?"

"That's one way to look at it," Captain McCord said. "Blood on her jacket and left in her car, hidden for months. Something doesn't add up."

"It does add up, sir. She left that jacket at the scene. We found Michael's blood in Leon's car, along with her blood. She fought against being taken and got a slight injury. Plus, she said she had Michael's blood all over her hands." He slapped his right palm on the table. "Whoever moved her car took the jacket, too. Which means that on the night of the murder, the wounded congressman was able to call someone else after Leon left with Erin."

Nicholas spoke up. "And tonight he called someone to kill her and to make sure we found that car."

"But still no sign of the murder weapon," McCord replied. "Maybe they'll gift us with that next time."

"I don't want there to be a next time," Chase replied.

McCord's grudging nod confirmed the obvious. "Okay, I can see that scenario about someone placing the jacket in the car. Fits right in with her being set up." He shook his head. "But we have to look at the facts and follow the evidence. So far, we know Erin Eagleton was at the murder scene and inside Leon Ridge's car, and now we have her car and a blood-caked jacket that matches the one she described to you."

Chase wanted to tell them about the things that didn't add up. "And someone brought that car to the safe house because they sent killers in first. They figured Erin and possibly Brooke would both be dead before we found the car."

"And that would have been that." McCord grunted and rubbed his face before he lifted off the corner of the table. "We need to beef up the search for the congressman. He can't get away with murder and attempted murder no matter where he hides. I hate to admit it, but he looks guilty of more than just corruption."

"He needs to step forward like a man," Chase retorted.

McCord's stare pinned Chase to the floor. "You've done a good job, but...you're too involved. Should have known it might come to this."

Chase couldn't argue with that. He was involved. He wouldn't let Erin become a scapegoat for a man who'd fooled a lot of people in the past. "Look, Captain, the evidence is mounting against Leon Ridge as possibly being an accessory to murder. We need to get him to talk again. I believe he's still hiding a lot, especially the part where he took Erin against her will."

The captain studied Chase for a moment. "Let me go back in and tell him we've found the car and the jacket. That's all he needs to know right now. Once the techs get back to us after examining the jacket, we might find something more to push at him."

Chase had to follow orders. "What can I do in the meantime?"

"Go home and rest," McCord suggested. "We'll make sure Miss Eagleton is placed in a new safe house."

Chase dug in his heels. "With all due respect, sir, I can't go home and rest."

McCord didn't bulge. "Zachary, you're running on fumes. That means you go home and rest up."

Chase nodded and left the room. But no way was he going to get any rest.

Erin didn't know where they were taking her. She'd been at K-9 headquarters all night and now she only knew she had to leave quickly and in the dead of night. Without Chase or Valor with her.

"Don't worry," Chase had whispered in a quick, cryptic tone. "I'll be watching out for you."

"But—"

"Just do as they say, Erin. We have to move you and...they think I'm going home to twiddle my thumbs."

But he wasn't. That's what he was trying to tell her.

"Don't get fired over me, Chase. I'm not worth it."

"Believe," he said. "Remember? We need to believe in each other and in God's grace and goodness. I'll make sure I know where the captain takes you."

She wanted to believe. She did have faith. Her faith had held her together even in her darkest moments. But faith without action was just a facade. Chase had shown her how to believe in another human being, to trust another person to help her. To trust him the way she had when they were so young and in love.

Could she go back out there without Chase and Valor by her side, guiding her and protecting her? Erin hated the shudder of fear curling against her spine.

"I'll be okay," she said, trying to remember the boy she'd loved long ago in the mature, handsome face she saw now.

"Yes, because this team is the best in the world." He winked at her and turned. But she saw something there in his eyes, just a flicker of awareness that seemed to light her from inside. Chase had turned into a good man and he was good at his job.

If he said he'd find her, he would. She had no doubt of that.

"Ready?" Nicholas asked, Max at his feet.

"I think so," she replied. "I travel light these days."

Except for the tremendous burdens she carried on her shoulders. So much baggage, she felt weighted down. Too many *if only*s and *might have been*s. If only she'd stayed that summer and gone off to college with Chase in the fall, things might have been so different now. If only she'd tried harder to get Michael to open up about what had him so upset, she might have been able to save him.

As she was smuggled into a waiting car, she had

one more *if only* to add to that list. If only she could be free again.

Completely free and clear to be near Chase again.

TWELVE

Erin didn't like this. While her new guards were nice and well trained, she missed Chase. John Forrester and Dylan Ralsey both seemed as capable as Chase and the others. These two hunks had adorable four-legged partners that were trained to attack and protect. She should feel safe.

She only felt lonely.

The house was plain and three-storied, one of those Georgetown brownstones that blended in with all the others around them. But it was apparently off the beaten path and so nondescript, no one would even notice she was here. The tall narrow house sat apart in what looked like an unoccupied row of four other side-by-side houses, far from the others on the street, probably to avoid any neighbors getting too close. Same as the last place.

Did Chase know where she was?

Would he really come for her or would he realize he was better off being taken off her protection detail? He'd come so close to being killed too many times, she wouldn't blame him for letting the other team members take over for a while. But he'd also saved her life several times.

Would these two officers do the same? Of course they would. They were handpicked by Captain Mc-Cord. The man might not believe her, but he sure took his duty to protect Erin seriously. Maybe because her powerful father was breathing down his neck. She'd even heard the president himself wanted this over. No more than she did.

Or maybe because Gavin McCord was every bit as good at his job as the team under him. If her father and their boss didn't give them all commendations after this was over, Erin sure would.

If this ever ended.

"Do you need anything, Miss Eagleton?"

Erin whirled from where she stood in front of an empty fireplace to find Dylan Ralsey and his dog, Tico, both staring at her. The man had straight dark inky hair and dark, almost black eyes to match, while the dog had dark fur around his ears and nose and a silky lighter brown coat that reminded her of Valor.

Erin glanced at the half-eaten piece of toast she'd left on a tray. "No, thank you. I'm fine."

"Did you sleep last night, ma'am?"

"Yes, I did." She hadn't, but that wasn't his problem.

"Would you like more coffee?"

She eyed the coffee carafe sitting by the tray on a nearby table. "I can get it myself. Would you like a cup?"

"No, I'm good. I'll be in the hallway if you need anything. And John and his partner, Guard, are at the back door."

"Got it, thanks," Erin said, not meaning to sound so harsh. Officer John Forrester and his German shepherd, Guard, were both just as serious as this one. And just as attentive.

But how could she explain that she was about to crawl out of her skin? How could she keep living her life like this, on the run for close to six months and still being stalked and shot at? Pursued? What next?

She'd been back in DC for little more than a couple of weeks and Jeffries was still coming at her. What could he possibly gain if everyone knew he was trying to kill her? Did he think eliminating her would save him, give him redemption, or maybe lessen his guilt?

Erin stood there and prayed for the Capitol K-9 Unit and all the team members who'd dropped everything to solve this case. She prayed for Chase and hoped he'd get the rest and peace he needed. She prayed for her father and Selena and everyone else who believed in her.

And she asked God to help her find the way. How could she end all of this and get on with her life, get on with her grief and, maybe, get to know Chase all over again?

Then she remembered something very clearly.

No one had ever found the murder weapon. She'd heard Chase and the others discussing that particular detail time and again.

It was hard to prove anything without the murder weapon.

"And I think I know where it might be," she whispered into the cold, dark fireplace.

But she wasn't sure how she'd ever get anyone to believe her or take her to that particular place.

Chase had been cleared to help watch the safe house. Now he was guarding the street behind the house, a plain brick three-story sitting away from the other homes on a quiet cul-de-sac. He knew the place since he'd brought an informant here once to be called as a witness in a drug lord's trial.

It had a front door and a back door with steps down to the small yard and a back-street entrance, and a basement entrance much like the last house. They usually kept the basement locked and off-limits just in case an occupant decided to bail out on them.

Which this particular occupant just might do.

Chase wouldn't blame Erin if she did run. They hadn't done a very good job of hiding her. Chase certainly hadn't done his job to the best of his ability.

But he couldn't shake the feeling that someone, somewhere was always watching and reporting back to Congressman Jeffries. It wouldn't be hard to pay a mole to tell the congressman their every move. Chase didn't have time to pursue that angle, but he had asked Fiona to keep eyes on everyone in and out of headquarters. Deliverymen, carriers, temps, anyone.

Fiona had managed to find the calls the congressman had made before he'd contacted 911. One number was a match to Leon's cell number. The other matched that of the man Chase had shot at the inn. Another tiny break.

Maybe they'd get a break on whom the congressman had watching them, too.

Meantime, he hoped to get Erin out of this city if this place was breached. He'd gone over the plan with the captain. But they all agreed that, sooner or later, this had to stop.

So he watched, knowing a team of the best K-9 officers had been assigned to guard her. During the day, that meant Dylan Ralsey and John Forrester. At night,

Deanna White and Tasha Lamant took over. All great at their jobs.

Chase was just glad to be involved. He and Valor waited in an unmarked car behind the house each day. He was to report anything he thought might be suspicious to those inside the house. Three days in and nothing.

Until today.

When he looked up a half hour before the shift change at dusk, he saw a man dressed in black moving up the stairs to the kitchen entryway. Chase didn't get out of his car, but he kept his eyes trained on the man. Valor's ear pricked up, but he remained as quiet as a church mouse.

He had to alert the officers inside, so he radioed Dylan.

Dylan listened and then replied, "We'll get her out of here."

"Wait." Chase lifted his binoculars and watched the man hovering on the tiny porch stoop, a package of some sort in his hands. What he saw sent a chill down his spine. "All of you need to get out of there. He's wiring the kitchen door with what looks like some sort of explosive."

Erin was learning to listen when the officers compared notes. She'd heard things over the past few days.

"No news on Jeffries, no sightings of him anywhere in the city. We've got eyes on his apartment in town and his estate, but we've heard he's long gone and out of the country. We've had reports from the FBI that they've done another sweep of both places."

"He won't come back to either residence. Too hot. He's probably in Switzerland or the Caymans by now."

"We might not ever find him. And with no murder weapon, we might not ever solve this case."

Where did that leave her? Erin wondered today while she waited for the changing of the guard. No word from Chase either.

If something didn't happen soon, she would have to find a way to get back out there on her own. It might be the only way she could stay alive to prove Harland Jeffries killed his son.

Then she heard Dylan talking on his phone. "We'll get her out of here."

After that, everything shifted into motion. One of the dogs started growling and both men went into action. Dylan rushed back to the living room with his dog, Tico, while Officer Forrester held his position at the front of the house, his partner's hackles raised. Then he said something into the radio he carried. "Got it. What's your location?"

Whom was he talking to?

"Front door about to be breached. Stay there. We'll get her out the back."

"What's going on?" Erin asked, already dreading the answer.

"Follow me, ma'am," Dylan answered, grabbing her by the arm to guide her toward the back of the house. Another noise and he slipped his weapon out of its holster.

"I think we have visitors at both entryways," he said into his radio. "I'll take care of our guest. Tico will escort us."

"Roger that," Officer Forrester shot back, his voice full of static. "Basement?"

"Sounds like. I'll get her out that way."

"Go. I got this."

Officer Ralsey signaled to Tico. "Go."

The big dog barreled toward the basement door and waited, then went ahead while Dylan got it open and took Erin down the narrow stairs.

"We're gonna get you out of here and when I open this door up to the street, Tico and I will make sure it's safe and then we need to run to the right. Got that?"

"Yes," Erin said, her heart rate increasing with each step they took. "What are you going to do?"

"I'm going to protect you from whoever is trying to get to you," Dylan answered in a no-nonsense voice. "Don't panic but they've wired this house to explode."

"A bomb?"

Dylan nodded and whispered, "We have to get you to safety. A car will pull up out back and no matter what, you need to get in that vehicle, understand?"

"Yes."

Erin wasn't surprised that she was being attacked again, but she sure wished Chase were here, too. She trusted these two men and she didn't want anything to happen to them, but…she and Chase seemed to have their own unspoken language.

Dylan had her at the basement door to the street now. Unlocking it, he peeped outside. Tico scratched at the door, his nose in the air. The dog went ahead, sniffing and growling.

"Ready?" Dylan asked, guiding Erin toward the door.

"Yes." But she wasn't ready. She wasn't ready at all.

Dylan turned to her. "Listen to me. This is very important. If anything happens to me or Tico, you keep running to the right up the street. You understand?"

"Yes, I mean, no. I won't leave you."

"You have to, Miss Eagleton. Just run to the right."

"Okay."

They crept out the door and up the concrete steps to the street. Erin stayed behind the tall officer, but Tico alerted and headed up the steps toward the back-door stoop, his growls and snarls vicious now.

A man stood on the stoop over them. Tico advanced and growled low. She gasped, causing the intruder to spot them.

"Stop," Dylan shouted to the intruder. "Stop right there or I'll shoot."

The man turned to run down the steps, a gun in his right hand. Halfway down, he stopped again. "This place is about to go up in smoke." And then he held up what looked like a cigarette lighter. Tico jumped forward, still growling. "Tell the dog to halt now or this place will blow. You need to give me the girl."

Dylan whispered to Erin, "On three, you run. Just run."

Then he rounded the wooden steps, his gun raised. "Put down your weapon and take your hand off that switch."

"Can't do that."

The intruder stood with the gun trained on Erin, his other hand holding the denotation device.

"The bomb squad and a SWAT team are headed this way," Dylan said in a calm voice. "And that K-9 officer will eat you alive before you ever activate that device."

"I'll take my chances," the nervous man said, his eyes now on Tico.

Dylan gave Erin a nod. "One, two, three—"

After that, everything happened so fast, Erin couldn't breathe. The intruder fired off a shot. Dylan shot back and she heard another shot. The man hit the button and then fell off the steps and into the street. Erin screamed and turned back, thinking the whole place was about to explode.

Dylan gripped his left shoulder and called to Tico. Blood was seeping between his fingers. "Run," he said to Erin on a weak breath. "Hurry."

Erin glanced around and saw Tico rushing down the stairs to guard the man who'd been shot. "No, I have to get you away—"

And then, she felt herself being lifted into the air. Another man, dressed in black. Grabbing her, dragging her toward a waiting van.

"Let me go." She kicked and screamed and tried to get out of his grip. More shots, but not from Dylan. Erin wasn't sure where they'd come from. The man holding her collapsed in front of her feet, his eyes open to nothing.

He was dead.

Erin scanned the street then turned back to where Dylan lay, still holding his bleeding shoulder. The basement door swung open and John Forrester and the other K-9 named Guard came running up the steps to the street. She could hear sirens off in the distance.

John glanced at her. "Go. Run!"

What about the bomb? She stared up at the door above them. A hissing sound filled the night and she smelled something acrid and chemical.

Then another hand on her. She swung around and came face-to-face with Chase. "Let's go," he said, dragging her up to the street.

A car sat idling beside the old fence. Chase opened the passenger side door. "Erin, get in. Hurry."

Chase! He'd been in on this.

She looked back at where they'd left Dylan and John and then she got inside the car.

Chase immediately radioed back for an update. "Ralsey, Forrester, report."

Nothing.

Chase stopped the car. "I'm going after them." But before he could get out, John Forrester appeared on the street behind them, holding up his wounded friend. Dylan grimaced but gave Chase a thumbs-up.

"Get her out of here," John called, waving them on.

They were a block away when the house exploded and a huge mushroom of flames and smoke filled the night air.

THIRTEEN

Chase kept checking Erin for signs of shock. "Hey, you still with me?"

"I'm okay," she said, her voice still and flat. "I'm okay."

Chase pulled out his cell. He'd warned Forrester and Ralsey about a possible bomb.

"I have to make sure they're all right." He pulled out his phone and waited for his contact to answer and then said, "Can you give me an update?"

Deanna White sounded winded. "Everyone is safe. Did you get the package out okay?"

Chase looked over at Erin. "Yes."

"Good," she said. "John's ears are ringing and Dylan's gunshot wound will heal. A through-and-through in his left shoulder." Another beat then she added, "And Captain McCord is surveying the scene. You are to proceed as planned."

He ended the call and put away his phone. "The two officers are okay. They know I have you."

Erin lifted up to stare over at him. "That's good, but where are we going now?"

"Out of the city," he said, his hands clutching the

steering wheel. He'd picked her up in an unmarked car and now he watched to make sure no one was tailing them. "But first, I want to take you back to headquarters with me. I need to interrogate Leon Ridge again, but I can't do that and worry about you, too."

"So I get to watch you work him over?"

He smiled at her dry humor. "No, you get to stay in the conference room, where we can all watch out for you."

"But won't your captain be mad that you took me away from the safe house?"

Chase shook his head. "He knows I took you. We planned for this. Did you see what happened back there? Erin, they've been coming after you for months. They were after you the night I found you and they found you at your father's heavily gated estate, and then the first safe house and at yet another safe house handpicked by Captain McCord. Enough is enough."

"I agree," she said, her hands together in her lap, her head down. "I agree. Every time I get shuffled to another location, I think about running again. And now I wish I had left. You can't be involved in this anymore."

"I've been involved since the night I found your necklace at the crime scene."

"Do you still think I killed him, even after Leon Ridge admitted Jeffries accidentally shot Michael?"

"I know you didn't kill Michael," he said. "I believe you, but the congressman and Leon don't want anyone else to know the truth. They don't want to admit that you were there that night. You won't be safe until we can force Jeffries's hand." He watched the dark road and then added, "I want to clear your name, Erin. No questions left, no regrets."

"And how do you suggest we do that?"

"I don't know yet, but…I'm starting with pinning Leon Ridge to the wall, and then after I've talked to him I intend to get you out of DC."

"Do you know more than you're saying?"

Fatigue dragged at him like a heavy fog, but he wouldn't give up. "No. I'm still trying to find a way to prove beyond a doubt that you are telling the truth. I believe the congressman accidentally killed his son and then when he realized you'd witnessed it, he panicked and refused to call the authorities. Then he decided to pin Michael's death on you to save his political career and to hide the corruption he's gotten away with for years. That's what I need to prove, Erin. That he's trying to frame you to save himself."

"Yes, he is," she said after a long sigh. "Chase, I appreciate how you're willing to help me, but we can't keep doing this."

"I don't much care about all of that right now," he said. "I'm taking you to what I consider to be a safe, secure place."

"Where?"

"I'd rather not say."

She hushed for a few moments and then asked, "Is this how I'm supposed to spend the rest of my life? I can't go into witness protection because I'm still a suspect of sorts. I've told the truth but with Jeffries in hiding, I might not ever be safe. I don't want to look over my shoulder anymore, Chase."

"You won't have to," Chase told her. "I've beaten a path over and over every lead, Erin. I've talked to anyone who might remember something from this investigation. I'm slowly building a case against Jeffries."

He let out a breath and continued. "We know he is

Juan Gomez's father. We know Michael made inquiries all that week regarding Juan's parentage and his father's possible involvement. We know someone killed Rosa Gomez on Jeffries's orders. And we've established that Tommy Benson snuck out of the foster home that night and saw Congressman Jeffries holding a gun. This whole chain of events—Rosa's murder, Michael's murder, the All Our Kids home being attacked and almost burned down, break-ins at the White House and attacks on Selena, the museum where Rosa's sister, Lana, was attacked, crooked aides being paid off and even using Danielle Dunne's mafia father coming after her as a means for a cover-up, and then Leon Ridge planting bombs to scare off Isaac Black—all of these things lead back to Congressman Jeffries."

Chase glanced at her. "We only need to piece together the part where you come in, and I think Leon Ridge will crack on that one, too. We need a little more time and I'll have it figured out." He shifted in his seat and checked the rearview mirror. "First, I'm going to sit down with Leon again. As soon as possible."

"Well, remember to ask Leon Ridge where he hid the murder weapon," she said, her tone firm and sure. "Better yet, take me with you since I have an idea that it's on the Jeffries estate somewhere. I'd like to watch Leon squirm when he figures out I'm alive."

Chase nodded on that. "Oh, don't worry. You will definitely go with me. I'm not letting you out of my sight. But you will not get to watch us interrogate Leon."

"As long as he confesses everything, I can live with that," she replied.

Chase wanted her to live for a lot more reasons than making Leon Ridge cave.

* * *

An hour later, Chase and Captain McCord sat in the interrogation room at the Capitol K-9 headquarters, both staring across the table at Leon Ridge. Ridge didn't look so hot. He was built like a linebacker, but his pallor spoke of being confined too much. Maybe prison life didn't agree with him.

Chase leaned forward. "I'm not going to waste time, Leon. We have a problem. Erin Eagleton is alive and in our custody. Her story matches yours in spots, but we need to make both versions match up to get the real story. If you have any hope of coming out of this with a lesser sentence, now is the time to spill it because Jeffries is still trying to kill her."

Chase halted and put his hands on the table. "Do you want another woman's death on your conscience?"

Leon looked blasé at first, but he started twitching. "What do you mean?"

Chase hit a palm on the table. "I mean, you're looking good for concocting this whole scenario. You'll be the fall guy for murder if Jeffries isn't located. And if Erin Eagleton is harmed in any way, her father will make sure you're not only in jail. He'll make sure you suffer for possibly aiding and abetting a fugitive. Suffer, Leon. Really suffer. Think about that."

Leon scratched his nose and sweated. "I told you, I don't know anything about Erin Eagleton."

But Chase saw something in his eyes. A sadness that pushed through the disregard that shouted at Chase. Chase decided to start with the one thing that had been bugging him. And this one thing might sway Leon. "Why did you have a picture of Rosa Gomez in your car, Leon?"

Leon's head came up and his face reddened with anger. "I don't know what you're talking about."

Too late to lie. The man had reacted too quickly to that question. McCord's gaze narrowed, but he didn't react. The captain sat as still as a rock.

Chase pulled out the picture from a folder. Covered in clear plastic, the aged photo showed a smiling Rosa standing in what looked like the garden at Jeffries's estate. "We found this underneath the front seat of your car. The same car you used to kidnap Erin Eagleton."

Leon strained at his handcuffs. "Did she tell you that?"

Chase refrained from screaming out his frustrations. He had to focus on this for Erin's sake. She was sitting in a guarded conference room across the hall right now.

"Erin? Yeah, she told us a lot of things. Said you helped the congressman out that night. Shot him with his own gun to make it look as if she'd done it and then you pushed her into your car with orders to kill her."

Chase lifted the picture and waited for a moment. Leon's demeanor had changed. He was jittery and visibly shaken.

Chase kept pushing. "Congressman Jeffries allegedly had an ongoing affair with Rosa and we have evidence that he hired someone to kill her."

Leon's eyes widened. "I don't know nothing about any of that."

Maybe not, but he kept staring at the picture of Rosa. "Did you know Rosa, Leon?"

Leon lowered his head and pushed a chained hand through his thinning hair. "Yeah, of course. I saw her around the estate. Nice lady."

"How nice?"

"What do you mean by that?"

McCord gave Chase the one-eyebrow-up frown. Probably wondering where Chase was going with this.

Chase tried again. "I mean, was Rosa nice to *you*? Did you ever eat in the kitchen, chat with her or discuss the weather or what a wonderful boss you both had?"

Leon's frown made him look as if he'd swallowed nails. "I liked her, yeah. She was good to me."

"Did the congressman know you two were close?"

A light of rage fused through the criminal's eyes. "What? What are you saying? What have you heard?"

McCord grunted. "I'd like to hear that myself."

Chase's stomach burned with the sure knowledge that he was on to something. "Did you have a thing for the congressman's secret lover, Leon?"

Leon went molten, his gaze firing a black hostility across the table. "I don't have to answer that."

Captain McCord stared at the picture and then looked at Leon. "I think maybe you should answer that since it might help your case." He glanced from Leon to Chase. "But you think about it while we step out for a break, okay?"

Chase didn't want a break, but the captain's scowl told him he'd better take one. Once they were out in the hall, he turned to McCord. "Sir, I think Leon had a thing for Rosa. If he did, then he might turn on Jeffries. I mean, what if he really did try to kill the congressman that night?"

McCord stood as silent and still as a statue. "That's a stretch, Chase. But I have to admit, you're making him sit up and take notice."

Chase nodded. "I'm going to check on Erin and then we'll go back in."

McCord looked through the one-way mirror to where

Leon sat staring at the picture Chase had left on the table. "Okay."

Chase hurried to find Erin. She was sitting curled into an office chair, a magazine open in her lap and Valor at her feet. When she saw him, she stood up, a questioning expression lighting up her face. Valor did pretty much the same.

"Hi." She slid her hands inside the pockets of her jeans.

"Hey." He moved toward her, wanting to touch her and hold her tight. Instead, he patted Valor on the nose. "We took a break, but…Leon's beginning to see the error of his ways."

"Has he corroborated what I've told you?"

"We're getting there." Chase moved an inch closer. "How you doing in here?"

She gave him one of her sweet smiles. "Valor and I are sharing a lot of secrets. He's a good therapist."

"Yeah, I tell him all of my troubles," Chase admitted. "And we compare notes on you, of course."

She leaned close. "All good, I hope."

Chase moved way too near, the floral scent enticing him. "We both think you're special. And…I gotta get back in there."

"Okay." She stepped back and pushed at her hair. "Chase, thank you."

Chase nodded and went back to grill Leon Ridge a little more. But he held being near Erin over his heart like a shield.

"Okay, so what's the deal, Leon?" he asked a couple of minutes later. "Tell us about Rosa and we'll get to the rest later."

Leon swallowed and shifted in his seat for a few more minutes, his expression changing from dark resistance to clear resolve. "All right, okay, so I cared about Rosa." He looked down at his big hands. "She was good to me and...he treated her like dirt."

"*He* being the congressman," Chase said.

"Yeah." Leon turned conversational. "After she had the baby, I tried to help her out. She didn't have much money and her only sister wouldn't have anything to do with her. She cried a lot and she was always tired. Didn't get much sleep with the boy always crying and needing attention. I felt sorry for her."

"So you didn't feel this way until after the child was born?"

Leon shook his head. "I treated her bad, too, at first. But then, I saw how he treated her, how he wouldn't even acknowledge the baby. His baby. So I started bringing her supplies and, sometimes, flowers and candy. I had to hide it from him, of course. But I got to know her and I liked her." He sniffed and looked down at the table. "I loved her."

"How did she feel about you?" Captain McCord asked.

"She cared about me, but she was afraid to...end things with him. She went to him right before she died, hoping to get some help for the boy. Juan was sick and even though she had nice presents from Jeffries, she could barely afford a doctor. I don't think he liked her asking for more money."

Chase exchanged glances with the captain. "I can see how being around each other and both of you having to take orders from a man like Jeffries could bring about a strong bond." Then he tapped his fingers on the steel tabletop. "Did you know they were going to kill her?"

"No, I swear I didn't or I would have stopped it. The man you killed at the inn, he pushed Rosa off that cliff. After that night, I wondered…and then everything happened so fast the night Michael died." Leon's vacant eyes went misty. "They didn't have to kill her, you know. She just needed more money. For the boy."

"You're right on that one," the captain said. "Which is why you shouldn't have to take the fall for a rich and powerful man who's probably sitting somewhere on a beach laughing at us."

McCord kept staring across the table. "And, Leon, if you think those suits who keep visiting you are here to save you, guess again. The DA can twist this to make a strong case against you even for Michael Jeffries's murder. You had motive and you had opportunity. Maybe you went to the estate to confront the congressman about Rosa's death and Michael got in the way. The congressman said he didn't see the shooter, so…he could easily pin it on you. You shot the congressman and you kidnapped Erin Eagleton and planned to kill her on his orders, right?"

"Yeah, right." Leon realized he'd just confessed. "I mean, he made me do all of it. I didn't kill Rosa or Michael, but the congressman had me shoot him and take the girl." He shook his head. "Erin Eagleton saw too much, knew too much."

Chase frowned at the fidgety criminal. Leon had just proved what Erin had known all along. "Leon, he's trying to kill a senator's daughter. A woman who hasn't done anything evil or criminal in her life. You can help us stop this."

Leon's glare had fizzled to a feeble frown. "I told you, I was trying to help the Eagleton woman. But she ran away from me. And I can't stop what's already been set in motion."

Chase started to stand, but the captain's hand held him in check. McCord leaned in toward Leon. "Maybe you can tell us where the murder weapon is. Anything to redeem yourself."

Sweat beaded on Leon's forehead. "I threw it away, after the woman ran." He lifted his head, his anger now directed toward the man who'd brought them all together. "It ain't right, but I'll go down for this, no matter what. I've got a target on my back. I'm already a dead man, so what does it matter what I say or do?"

Captain McCord scrubbed his hand down his chin. "So…what have you got to lose? Do something decent, Ridge. Tell us everything you know. Avenge Rosa's death and help us save Erin Eagleton."

Leon Ridge glared at the captain, but the flare of rage returned to his eyes. "I don't know what to do."

Chase pushed his chair back so hard, it fell to the floor. "He's going to kill her because she was there that night, but if your story matches hers, we can help you. We can go from there."

Leon lowered his head and stared at his handcuffs. "Okay, all right, I'll tell you the rest. So she was there that night. The congressman accidentally shot his son. That's the truth. And the woman did see it happen." He stopped, took a deep breath, his beady eyes going dark. "Jeffries panicked when Erin Eagleton wanted him to call for help and then he kind of went haywire and decided he needed to pin this murder on Miss Eagleton. He ordered me to shoot him to make it look like he was a target, too, and he ordered me to take Miss Eagleton out and kill her after I shot him."

"And where did you take her?" the captain asked, disgust sharpening his question.

"I stopped somewhere way back in the woods up near a hill."

"Did you shoot *at* her?" Chase asked.

Sweat beaded on Leon's upper lip. "Maybe. I mean, man, I had to do my job. It's always about cleaning up messes, you know." He leaned back in a slump. "But she got away, and she kept running." He finally looked up and straight into Chase's eyes. "And I let her run. I let her get away. I didn't want to kill her."

Chase kicked at his chair again. "That's some comfort then, isn't it?"

Leon gulped and glanced around as if someone might be listening. "The thing is—I haven't heard from Jeffries, but I know he's watching me. He must have found someone else to do his dirty work after you killed the man who murdered Rosa. And after you took me into custody." He shrugged. "Being in jail is the only thing keeping me alive right now."

Chase left the room and headed across the hall to Erin. "He told us just about everything."

Her eyes grew wide. "Thank goodness for that. Now what?"

"Now I take you to another safe place."

He hoped.

They were at a small cabin deep in the woods. She hadn't recognized any signs or markers since he'd taken the back roads in the wee hours. The night was black, with dark clouds looming overhead. The sticky air shouted for release. Lightning danced off in the distance, hiding the coming dawn. Chase had picked a perfect spot. Even if she wanted to leave, Erin would only wind up lost in the woods. A shiver of apprehension climbed up her backbone and caused her neck muscles to tighten. She didn't want to go back into the woods. So she turned and tried to focus on being here with Chase, safe and away from the evil that seemed to follow her.

A muted lamp on a small desk spotlighted the sparse, clean cabin. Paneled walls, a huge fireplace and old but comfy-looking furnishings filled the quaint space, along with an efficiency kitchen that held only the essentials. All flannel and wood without a trace of feminine influence. A hunting cabin. She did detect the slight scent of furniture polish and fabric freshener, however.

"So you get the bedroom down the hall and I'll bunk out here in the den," Chase explained. "Valor will guard you. He'll sleep at the foot of the bed."

"And who will guard you?" she asked, pushing at her always-messy hair.

He stopped and held his hands on his hips. "I'm trained to guard myself."

She wondered about that. Did he have anyone on his side? He never talked about his personal life. She didn't dare ask about his family, but she knew Chase had always been close to his parents. He was prickly tonight, on edge.

"Are you hungry?" he asked now.

"No."

"The kitchen's stocked with crackers, cheese and some fruit, soup, sandwich meat. Sodas and coffee and plenty of water."

"Someone knows we're here?"

"Someone brought supplies."

"Oh, I see. You thought of everything."

Chase roamed around the cabin while Valor lay in front of the cold fireplace with eyes that followed his partner. "Let's talk about locating the murder weapon, Erin."

Oh, that had to be the reason for the mood. That and another harrowing experience that had almost gotten his team members killed. When she'd talked about searching for the missing gun the congressman had used to shoot Michael, instead of asking questions, he'd gone quiet. But now he knew she'd been telling the truth. Still, he had to keep pushing. He'd kept her at headquarters until it was safe to travel again.

Sitting down because she didn't know what else to do, she said, "I know the murder weapon is still missing."

"That's right," he said, finally taking a stool by the fireplace to sit near the sofa, where she sat with her legs curled up. "Leon said he threw it away somewhere in the woods. Is that what you remember?"

Erin nodded at that analysis. "He's one of the top dogs on the congressman's staff. Always hanging around, slipping in and out of rooms. He knows where all the bodies are buried and he knows that estate inside and out. He could probably take you right to the place where he hid the gun."

"Did you notice anything odd when he forced you into his car?"

Wondering why Chase asked that question, she said, "No. It was dirty. Lots of old food wrappers. I mostly watched for road signs and a way out. I remember the gun, though."

She closed her eyes for a moment. "The congressman had blood all over his hands and I saw blood on the gun, too. Michael's blood." She lowered her head and closed her eyes. "I've tried to block it out of my mind, but…it keeps coming back."

Chase thought back over what he knew. "Michael was shot at close range. We know the congressman had blood on his clothes. His and Michael's. We thought because he'd tried to help Michael."

"He didn't." She pushed at her hair. "Splatters. He had splatters from when the gun went off."

Chase's gaze locked with hers. "Let's go back to Leon's involvement." He came over to sit down beside her. "So where do you think he hid the gun?"

His nearness only reminded Erin of how much she'd missed him. He looked tired and…aged. But his question shouted out the doubt he still had about her involvement in that horrible night.

"I don't know for sure," she admitted. "I'm guessing. But the congressman was a gun advocate and an experienced hunter and marksman. He valued all of his weapons, some of them antique and expensive. He would have realized Leon might still have the gun, and he would have asked Leon about it so they'd have all their bases covered. If Leon hid it in the woods, the congressman wouldn't be happy about that."

Pushing up off the sofa, she pivoted at the fireplace and turned to Chase. "The congressman would want to get that gun back because he's that arrogant and panicky. Leon probably planned to go back and get it when things cooled down."

"Why wouldn't he just throw it in the river or hide it away from the estate?"

"Leon could use the murder weapon to blackmail the congressman." She stared at the cold fireplace. "I think that in all the commotion, Leon injured Congressman Jeffries worse than either of them had planned. The congressman passed out and he realized later that the gun was gone. Leon had it." She glanced down at the dark socks covering her feet. "He must have gone into a panic, but I'm sure he came up with another lie in case he had to answer questions regarding the gun."

"So maybe you're right on the blackmail thing. Leon says he tossed the gun, but maybe he knows exactly where it is. He has motive. He was in love with Rosa Gomez."

Erin wondered how she hadn't seen this before. "Michael used to complain about him hanging around, always flirting with the women on staff and bragging about his new car, new motorcycle and things such as that. Leon liked to talk up his position on the congressman's staff. He impressed the lesser-paid help."

"We found a photo of her under the seat of Leon's car along with the traces of Michael's blood and your blood."

"And you're just now mentioning this to me?"

He got up and came to stand in front of her. "I haven't had a spare minute over the last few days to discuss anything with you. But Leon told us a lot last night."

Erin accepted that and remembered to be grateful for even the smallest things. "Well, you're here now and I appreciate that and how you're working so hard to help me," she said, her emotions crashing with the same intensity as the growing storm rumbling all around the cabin.

Chase stood a foot or so away, his gaze tugging at her, his eyes searching her face. "Yes, I'm with you now." Then he reached a hand around her waist and tugged her close. "I don't want to be without you ever again."

"I'm here," she said on a whispered plea while she forgot their conversation, forgot everything but Chase. "Believe in me, trust me. I need to know you can do that, Chase, no matter what."

"Let me show you, then."

Erin welcomed the closeness, accepted his gentle kiss with a sigh. And then, she was in his arms, her hands moving over his jawline and into his soft, clipped hair.

Outside, the rain began to fall. Chase pulled away to stare down at her. "This is dangerous. It's late. Maybe you should try to get some sleep."

"Yes." Forcing herself out of his arms, Erin took a calming breath. "You, too."

His hand on her wrist tugged her back around. "Erin, I promise you I will find Harland Jeffries. And when I do, I'll make him tell the truth."

"I know you will," she said, taking his hand in hers and lacing their fingers together. "I just don't want you to die doing it."

FOURTEEN

A couple of days later, Chase and Erin were back to business and skirting around the pull that kept the air between them charged with lightning bolts of awareness. But after going over the woods behind the estate, the crime-scene techs hadn't found the gun that had killed Michael Jeffries.

Chase broke the news to Erin as yet another rainy day turned into a stormy night. "No news on the gun, but we won't give up. If you think of anything—"

"Leon took me out the back way. That much I remember. Take *me* out there, Chase. Maybe I can find the spot."

Chase listened to Erin's emphatic plea again but disagreed. "That is not going to happen."

"Leon has admitted the congressman told him to kill me." She shrugged and held her hands down.

"Yes, and in a court of law, Jeffries's lawyers could twist that to make it look like you shot Michael and got away with Leon, and they could make it look as if you two are trying to frame the congressman."

"That's ridiculous. I've only been in the same room with Leon Ridge maybe four times in my life and we were with other people. I've never had a decent conversation with the man and I sure don't like him now."

"I understand that, but high-powered lawyers can make things stick even when they're ridiculous."

"What about all the other evidence?"

"It should hold. That and your testimony coupled with Leon's confession should be enough." He shrugged. "But we need all of it. If we can locate Jeffries and get a confession from him, this will all be over. But…that's asking for more than we might ever find."

Erin toyed with the zipper on her hoodie. "I wish I could find something more substantial to add. My memories are fuzzy, but I'm sure there's a missing link I've forgotten."

Chase stood near the window, the habit of checking outside making him antsy. "They know you're alive, Erin. And they're scrambling to cover their tracks because they have to believe you've told us the truth. Even your memories are dangerous."

She got up off the couch and stalked across the cabin like a mad feline. They'd been holed up here for two days and he'd seen every mood of Erin Eagleton.

She paced and sighed, stared into the cold fireplace and sat in an old armchair and read paperback books. Then she fumed and studied the notes in that little notebook she guarded like a hawk. Somehow, she'd managed to keep the mangled, frayed thing with her no matter how fast she had to run or whom she had to hide from. He wanted to take it and read it, but Chase was afraid it might contain more than just the details of her trauma.

His head came up. "Erin, what kind of things do you write in that pocket journal?"

She whirled, her hand checking the old cotton hoodie she wore. "Dates, events, thoughts. Mrs. Appleton gave it to me along with an ink pen. She saw me scribbling on a napkin. Told me to use the notebook as a journal." She shrugged. "She didn't even know my real name or why I was running, but she knew I needed to remember."

Erin had always loved her journals. And her doodles. He'd figured it was more personal than informative. More about Jeffries's unethical deals than the night of the murder.

"Have you actually gone over it?"

"Not too much until now. I've been busy trying to stay alive." Glancing toward the door, she said, "Every place you've brought me, I've thought of running. Just leaving it all behind. I've certainly written about that in my journal. I'm afraid to remember, Chase. Does that make sense?"

He wondered what she'd recorded about him. Maybe she was afraid to let him see that, too.

"You've been through a lot. Maybe that's why you've been hesitant to read your notes."

They looked at each other for a split second.

"Let *me* see that notebook," Chase said. "Maybe together, we can piece things into place."

Erin reached in her pocket and pulled it out and handed it to him. "I *have* looked over my scribbled notes several times while we've been here, but it's mostly what I could remember that first night at the bed-and-breakfast."

"We need to read it together and compare notes," he said. "With any investigation, you always follow the evidence, Erin. We have evidence. Just not enough."

She gave him a hopeful glance. "Anything to find

the last piece. Jeffries's gun. If Leon tossed it, it's in those woods somewhere."

Chase wondered how she could be so certain that the gun was hidden near the Jeffries estate, but his gut was burning, so he went with her theory for now. What did he have to lose?

An hour later, Chase's eyes stung with fatigue and his mind was boiling over with too many details that didn't add up.

"I told you this notebook has everything I could find regarding what I believed to be his hidden corruptions—"

"And those notes back up what we have on him," Chase interjected. "We need more. One tiny gem of evidence. Something that can substantiate your claim that Leon had the gun. He could always change his tune on that."

Erin grabbed the notebook back from Chase and began searching again. She went back to the beginning and studied each page, her eyes flashing with an intensity that had him worried.

"I ran and ran after I got away from Leon Ridge," she said. "It didn't seem as if he took me too far." She studied her scrawled words. "I found the Appletons' house in the middle of the night, and they took me in and gave me food and clothes."

She checked the first few pages. "My notes don't even make any sense to me."

Chase watched her, his heart aching for this incredible, brave woman. A woman he'd tried to put out of his mind for most of his adult life. But here she sat, back in his life and fighting for her innocence and her freedom. He wanted to help her, to prove she was telling the truth. He had a new hope for them, too, after seeing her doodles and notes.

She'd mentioned how he'd found her.

Chase is back in my life. It's amazing and scary, but if anyone can save me from this, Chase will.

He'd seen other notes about him, but she'd glazed over those like a bird fluttering away from danger. She didn't want him to see that part of her scribbling.

"I *was* right," Erin said on a little squeal that brought him out of his daydreams. "Here."

She sank back and pointed to some doodles on the third page of the lined notebook. "See that little box in the corner of this page?"

Chase nodded. "Yes. I didn't notice that much before. I thought maybe it was the Appletons' farmhouse."

"I forgot about even drawing it," she said. "But now I remember why I drew it."

"And?"

"Leon Ridge used the congressman's gun to shoot him in the shoulder," she said. "I saw that up close because Leon held on to me while he shot the congressman."

"Right, but you said Leon still had the gun when he forced you into the car, and he admitted that."

"The old square barn," she said, pointing to the little doodle. "The congressman had most likely been at the back of his property on a shooting range and that's why he had the gun with him that night. He and Michael used to go out there after work a lot. There's an old barn back there."

"Are you sure?"

"I drew that box while I was reliving the horror of that night." She turned to face Chase. "Leon held the gun on me until we got out to the woods, and he would have shot me with it, if I hadn't maimed him enough to get away." She jabbed a finger at the box. "Chase, I ran right past the barn, but I remember him firing at me in the dark. I heard the bullet hitting wood a few feet from my head. This little square is that barn. It has to be."

Chase wanted to celebrate with her, but he had to be sure. "So you're saying we might find a slug embedded somewhere in the wood?"

"Yes. Yes." She got up and moved around, excitement in her eyes. "And possibly the gun around there somewhere."

"We didn't search too far back in the woods that night," Chase said. "We focused on the scent we picked up that took us to the foster home. We didn't even know you were missing until the next day."

He stood to touch a hand to her cheek. "Erin, it's been six months since that night. Leon could have easily gone back to the scene to make sure he covered his tracks. Our techs haven't found anything out there."

She looked dejected and then shot up again. "But we can at least check it out, right? I mean, they might have looked all around the barn but they didn't know about the bullet hitting the wood. Have them look again. Let me go with them."

Chase jotted his own notes. "It's worth a shot, but you're not going."

She didn't look happy about that.

Chase went back over everything to keep from kissing her.

"We had no idea until last month when that boy— Tommy Benson—said he saw the congressman with the gun, that the congressman had used his own weapon, or we would have checked him that night for gunshot residue." He thought back over the evidence. "Michael's sweater and entry wound revealed what we call 'stippling,' which is soot and gunpowder burns that show the victim was shot at close range."

"Yes," she said, moving her head in agreement. "Michael and his father struggled, and his father grabbed the gun and held it to Michael's stomach." She put her hands to her mouth, her eyes going dark with terror. "Then Leon held me with one hand, and he shot the congressman from about fifteen feet away, maybe. They both shot that weapon."

Chase pulled out his phone and called Fiona. "Let's check once more. If we find the gun, we might also find some blood embedded in the barrel and maybe even the inner workings. We'd have to dismantle it, but it might be worth a shot."

"Chase, slow down. I'm working as fast as I can," Fiona said in an instant greeting. Chase pictured her red hair standing up in tufts stiffened by a substance they were all too afraid to ask about. "Got all that. What do you need from me?"

"Erin's jacket. It's too late to prove there was any GSR on it, but it tested positive for her blood and Michael's."

"Yes, we confirmed that—no gunshot residue but her blood and Michael's. Next?"

"The congressman's clothes contained bloodstains, right? But were they tested for GSR?"

It had been chaos that night and it was a long shot, but maybe someone had checked for GSR on his clothes after he was taken to the hospital.

Fiona mumbled to herself and then replied, "Okay,

according to the lab report, yes. Traces of GSR on his jacket and shirt, and his blood and Michael's on his clothes. We believed the gun powder residue came from the congressman being shot."

"Thank you, Fiona," Chase said. "How are things?"

"Good for you," Fiona retorted. "General Meyer told everyone to keep working on finding the truth. And she said to leave you and Erin alone for now."

Chase closed his eyes and sent up a silent prayer. The savvy general knew where he was keeping Erin. The whole team did and they were guarding the woods all around this place.

But due to his stint with the Secret Service, General Meyer *knew* Chase. That made his job easier and gave him the confidence to stay the course.

"Thanks for that information," he said. He ended the call and turned to Erin. "They found GSR on the congressman's clothes."

Erin squealed again. "So that proves he used the gun, right?"

"Yes and no. No one tested his hands because at the time we didn't know he'd touched the murder weapon. Now we do, of course."

She pushed at a cushion. "And he didn't volunteer that information."

"If he'd already been shooting the gun earlier that night, he'd have plenty of GSR on his clothes *and his hands*. But now he can deny all of that and keep pinning the murder on you."

"But Leon said he accidentally shot Michael and I saw him shoot Michael. So it's his words against Leon's and mine." Erin got up and ran her hands through her hair. "Tommy Benson also saw him with a gun."

"His lawyers would dispute that twenty ways to tomorrow." Chase followed her and turned her around. Valor watched them and waited for his cue. When none came he settled back to stare at them.

"Hey," Chase said, his hands moving through her hair. "It's not all bad news. If a slug is buried in that old barn wood, we need to find it and match it to the type of small-caliber gun we believe was used. A lot could go wrong, but it would be another piece of the puzzle."

Erin looked up at him with trusting eyes. He'd fought hard to earn that trust. And he'd tried to stay out of any kind of emotional tangle while he searched for answers. But being here with her 24/7 was both a joy and a challenge.

"Hey," she said. "How are *you*? I mean, really?"

He tugged her into his arms. "Right now? I'm good."

He put the investigation away and took another kind of risk. He pulled her into his arms and kissed her, slow and easy and with a deliberate gentleness so she'd feel that he would never leave her again.

Erin sighed against him and returned that same gentleness. He could tell she wanted to be in his arms.

Then she lifted away, her eyes dark with longing. "Chase, I want this to be over so we can…begin again."

"Me, too," he said, bringing her back. "Me, too."

Two nights later, Chase's cell phone buzzed. He got up from his spot on the couch and grabbed it, sleep making him sluggish. Valor sat up, always ready for some action.

"Zachary, we got trouble."

Nicholas Cole. Nicholas and Adam Donovan were helping to guard the perimeters around the cabin.

"Armed men combing the pasture and headed for the woods."

Chase was up and at the window. Valor followed suit. "Who and how many?"

"I can't tell. Looks like some sort of SWAT team but only a few. Maybe three or four." Nicholas paused and then said, "I don't think they're friendly."

A sinking feeling hit Chase in his solar plexus. "How did they get this far?"

"Waited and watched," Nicholas said. "It's dark and hard to see anything. Max alerted. They could be headed to…the other house on the property, too. But we won't let them get that far."

Chase went cold. With Valor like a shadow on his heels, he hurried to the bedroom and woke Erin. She sat up in a shot, her eyes wide. "Have they found us?"

"Someone's possibly nearby or at my parents' house."

"We're on your parents' land?"

"Yes," he replied, not bothering to explain. "Get dressed."

She stood up and shook her hair out. "I am dressed."

She slept in her clothes out of habit. A good thing she did, too. Even with the warm temperatures outside, Erin clung to her old hoodie and jeans like a shield. He remembered her wearing classic, preppy clothes before, but Chase didn't try to stop her quirky wardrobe habits now. Whoever that was would be here pretty soon. He prayed they didn't hurt his parents.

"Stay here while I check the front yard," he said, hurrying to the window in the other room. "Stay," he said to Valor. The eager dog settled and watched Erin's every move.

Why had he thought this was a good idea?

Too late to worry about that now. He had to get her to safety and go check on his parents. But when his phone buzzed again, Chase stopped and stared.

Captain McCord's number flashed like a laser across his phone screen.

"Sir," Chase said, his tone full of resolve.

"Kid, you need to move her again." A long heave of breath. "I have to admit, you sure picked a good hiding place this time. Took a few days for them to figure it out."

"But they keep coming."

"Yes, and I just found out why. Seems someone on Jeffries's staff—what's left of his staff—hired the same security company as Erin's father did."

Chase rubbed his forehead with two fingers. "A mole? That would explain why we never found the intruder who came into Erin's room. Our dogs would have been familiar with the scents already, too."

He heard a grunt of agreement. "Yeah, well, too late to discuss the variables now. I'm with your parents. They're safe. Just sit tight and we'll take care of your family."

Chase lowered his head, his gaze on the coming storm. "I'll do my best, Captain."

McCord grunted. "We've got your back on this. I should have had your back from the first day."

"It's okay, sir." Chase hung up and turned to get back to Erin. Then he heard Valor's low, aggressive growl, followed by angry barking.

Chase hurried to the back of the cabin.

Erin wasn't in the bedroom. The bathroom door stood open. Empty.

Valor stood on his hind legs, scratching at the heavy curtains over the window.

Chase rushed to the curtains and pulled them back. The window was partially open, the screen gone. Had Erin gone through this window? Had she decided to run again?

He stared out into the rain. Nothing.

He turned to check the room. Erin had left. And she'd taken her hoodie and her notebook.

The shock hit Chase like a battering ram.

Even after everything they'd been through, she still couldn't trust him? She'd walked away from him long ago while he'd been willing to fight, and now they were reliving history but in a much more dangerous way. If she'd run from him now after everything they'd been through together, maybe they weren't meant to be in each other's lives after all. She still couldn't trust him enough to believe in him, and this time her lack of trust could get her killed.

The pain he'd held in his heart for so long came back to Chase with a sharp slap.

She should have waited to see who was out there. Maybe she'd never truly trusted him and she'd only been waiting to escape—from him. Maybe Erin Eagleton just didn't need anyone to protect her and love her. Or she didn't want him in her life again, even if it meant saving her life.

Sick at heart, he radioed back to Nicholas while he worked to open the window wide. "I think Erin's on the run again. She's gone and I can't find any evidence that she was forced to leave."

Nicholas started shouting. Dogs started barking. "Go. We'll catch up."

Chase and Valor were already out the window.

FIFTEEN

Chase stalked through the trees, the dark woods he'd roamed as a child suddenly sinister and dangerous. In spite of his best efforts, Erin had become too afraid to stay with him. He'd tried so hard to protect her, and yet again he'd failed. Would he always be that country boy who'd had a chance at a life with her and missed it?

They were reliving history, but this time neither of them wanted it to end this way. He'd let her get away once and now he regretted that even more. She was in danger but she didn't want to let him help her, maybe because she'd never believed in him. So many times she'd talked about running, but he'd convinced her that he'd take care of her. But he hadn't done that.

Erin was better off without him after all since he hadn't done a good job of protecting her. But he'd keep doing that job tonight, so he put his personal feelings aside and concentrated on protecting the person they'd all worked so hard to shield.

He followed Valor into the thunder and lightning of yet another round of storms. A heavy rain hit at them, but Valor never stopped pushing through the woods. Would they be too late to help her?

His cell buzzed. Chase held it close.

"Location?" Captain McCord shouted over the clash of thunder.

Chase named the area. "The trail behind the cabin. Headed toward the river."

"We're spreading out," McCord replied. "We'll back you up and meet up with you on the dirt lane."

Back him up.

The captain was doing his job. Once this was over, Chase would probably be suspended or fired for messing this up. What then? All of his hopes and dreams had failed, and he'd have to start from scratch.

And the worst of it. He'd lose Erin. Again.

The rain slashed at him like a whip. The sky raged its own pain. Chase ignored the sharp needles of rain and kept trudging behind Valor, his mind churning with another kind of anger.

But somewhere in his tormented mind, his faith caught hold.

Maybe sometimes people had to be apart for a reason. He was stronger now, trained to protect and serve. He was tight with his team members and they'd all rallied around helping Erin, even when they'd doubted her.

Maybe God put you in this exact place at this time to save the woman you love. The woman you were meant to be with.

"Suffering produces perseverance, and perseverance, character, and character, hope."

The verse from Romans shot through Chase's mind like a bolt of lightning. He couldn't give up hope now. Now was the test of truly finding the courage he needed to do what he had to do. He'd save Erin, no matter the outcome, no matter what the future brought. That was his first duty. Save the one in danger.

Determination and a need to succeed caused him to push through the woods. Valor was on the scent, his nose in the air, the hairs on his neck and back bristling.

"Find her, boy."

When he heard other dogs barking, Valor whirled on the trail. Chase gave him full rein. "Where are you taking us?"

And then Chase heard a motor cranking and the roar of a movement through the trees.

Back toward the cabin they hurried, Valor leading the way. When the motor's whine came to a stop, Chase feared the worse. Erin must have taken the four-wheeler his dad kept at the remote hunting cabin. But then he thought he heard another sound. A vehicle cranking? And then, the muffled sound of a gunshot.

He urged Valor on, both of them running now.

He ran right smack up on Captain McCord and his German shepherd, Glory, followed closely by Brooke Clark and Mercy. Chase halted Valor and glanced around. No sign of Erin. When Valor alerted toward the trail, Chase almost let the big dog keep going.

But he held back. "Have you seen her, sir?"

The captain took off his wet cap and scratched his head. "She's gone. They used a four-wheeler to breach the trail by the river. Must have doubled back here while we were back there."

"What do you mean?" Chase asked, adrenaline shooting through him. "From what I could tell, she left on her own."

The captain gave him a surprised glare. "I don't think so. She didn't run away, Chase. Someone took her. And we're almost certain some of those involved were on the team who pretended to protect her at her father's house."

Chase's whole system changed course. Erin wasn't the one at fault here. He was. She kept reminding him he needed to believe in her. Had he failed at that, too?

"What happened?" he asked while Valor sat waiting. Chase didn't think his heart could pump any faster. "I heard the four-wheeler cranking in the woods."

Isaac Black stalked up, wet and fuming with frustration. His beagle, Abby, lowered her nose, her long ears brushing the mud. "They used the off-road vehicle to get her here and then took her out in a big van, Chase. Happened so fast, threw all of us off guard."

Chase slapped at the raindrops on his face. "I'm going after them." He'd track that van clear across the country if he had to.

"And how do you plan on doing that?" Captain Mc-Cord asked, sympathy in the question.

"Did we get a good description, a license plate?" Chase asked, dread weighing him down.

"I got a partial on the plates and the van was black, nondescript and long. No side windows." Isaac pointed toward the muddy road. "Already put out a BOLO. And we took down one of them. He's dead."

"So let's go over the scene," Chase said, walking Valor along the muddy tracks leading from the woods to the road. "They must have parked here behind those trees."

"Tracks lead from that area to the road," Isaac said.

"The rain's gonna wash away any evidence we might find," the captain called. "Do your best to find any trace you can before it's too late. We've got patrols out, watching for the van, and we've got ears to the ground. We've alerted Senator Eagleton about the security company. And we've sent team members and a cruiser to his house."

"Get someone out to the Jeffries estate," Chase said, his gaze sweeping the woods. If Jeffries had Erin, he'd probably try to kill her father and her, too. Unless he planned to take her hostage long enough to get away.

"You think *he* took her there?" Adam Donovan asked.

"Yes, I think he took her and yes, he might have taken her back there," Chase retorted, his impatience etched in a solid fear for Erin's safety. "He's been after her for six months and somehow, he's known our every move. He must have paid a pretty price to lure someone from that security team to his side."

The captain's expression sizzled with rage. "I think he knows too many people who have access to information that should have been kept quiet." He marched up to Chase. "What has she told you, Zachary? Anything that might shed some light on where he'd take her?"

"She wanted to go to Jeffries's estate," Chase said. "She remembered some more details of that night. Leon Ridge might have tossed the gun near an old barn on the back of the property."

"We can interrogate him again," Captain McCord said. "But he's pretty much told us everything. Of course, he could be lying about how he got rid of the weapon."

Chase nodded on that. "I had every intention of talking to Ridge again after she remembered the old barn. He didn't take her far from the crime scene."

"Do you want another go at him?" the captain asked.

Chase stared into the night, torn between going after Erin and trying to get the truth out of Leon Ridge. "No. I want to find Erin. Just see if he'll come clean on where he might have hidden that gun. If Jeffries knows the gun is still missing, he'll want to clean up that loose end right along with killing Erin."

SIXTEEN

Erin sat in the dark, inside the big cold van, and hoped Chase would find her soon. They'd blindfolded her and tied her hands, but after they'd stopped on a dark road in the middle of nowhere, they'd removed the covering from her eyes. She had a bad feeling her journey through this nightmare was about to be over.

He'd kill her.

The congressman had pursued her since that night, sending assailant after assailant, and now she'd run out of time. Not surprisingly, she'd recognized the voice of one of the men who'd been waiting when she came out of the bathroom. They'd forced her through that window with the threat of killing Chase and his family.

The man who'd whispered those threats while he held a gun to her ribs had been on her father's security team. A mole who'd probably been sent to kill her at her father's estate and at all the other locations where she'd been kept. It all made sense now. They'd been watching her since the night she'd run away.

Chase, I love you.

She wished she'd said those words. Tonight, she'd

had a chance, but they'd circled and backed away, too afraid to take things to the next level.

Now she sat here in the dark, lost and afraid. Chase didn't know they'd forced her. He probably thought she'd just left again.

He found you once. He'll find you again.

Dear Lord, I'm so tired. I've tried to stay strong. I need to let this burden go and let You take over.

Erin squinted into the storm. She could find the strength to run one more time. She had to fight until her last breath. She owed that to Michael and…to Chase.

As the darkness surrounded her and the two men who'd abducted her paced back and forth outside the van, Erin remembered her shock that night. She'd almost blacked out a couple of times, especially when she'd realized the congressman truly had gone mad. Had she heard something somewhere in that fog of horror, something she'd blocked out? Maybe she'd remember some other detail that could help her.

She started crying and hated herself for doing it, but she'd reached the point of no return. "Enough," she whispered. "Enough."

She had to remember Chase and how they'd somehow found each other again. *We tried to stay apart, but God brought us back together.* Surely that had to mean something.

If I ever break free from Harland Jeffries, I will find you and I will never let you go again.

That silent promise to Chase echoed inside her head while she waited for whatever came next. Her pledge to Chase gave her the burst of strength she needed to survive.

But then a long black car pulled up and a man got out.

Erin's pulse slammed against her temple, her heart rate rushing ahead so fast, she felt dizzy. She would run one more time to get away from this man. She had to try.

One of the goons opened the door for the man. He leaned in, a dark smile on his haggard face.

"There you are," he said, concern in his voice, censure in his eyes. "Are you hungry? I suspect you didn't have time for dinner."

"I don't have an appetite." She stared at the dark, wet night.

"Erin, you need to keep up your health," Congressman Jeffries said. "Life is too short to become malnourished."

Erin stared into his gleaming eyes and prayed her life wouldn't be cut short tonight.

Captain McCord stood with most of the team around him. They'd all been brought in with their K-9 partners after McCord had called Chase to tell him they'd located the van that had taken Erin. It was parked on a logging lane behind the Jeffries estate. Small hope, but it was a start.

While Chase and a couple of others searched the Jeffries estate and the woods, the rest were going to guard the one person who might be able to find the missing murder weapon.

Leon Ridge.

He wasn't happy about this field trip. "Y'all are using me as a decoy. He's gonna kill me. He knows I hid the gun because I tried to kill him with it. Now you're protecting the woman and putting me out here with a bull's-eye on my back."

"Shut up," Adam Donovan said. "You made some

bad choices and that's why you're standing here. Help us out and see where it goes from there."

Chase checked his weapons and made sure Valor's protective vest was securely buckled. Valor sat still, his ears up and his eyes watchful.

"Come on, boy," Chase said to the eager canine. "We're going to find our favorite person." Then he took off with Valor along the trail toward the woods. Being with Erin again had brought out something else he'd tried to hide. He loved Erin. He would always love her. But he had to get this case done and out of his system before he could tell her that. He should have told her tonight when they'd been so close. He'd believed she'd left again when she'd been taken. When would he learn that she loved him, too? That she needed him to believe in her, too?

Taken once by social status and prestige. Taken tonight by an evil man who wanted to hang on to both those things. Chase would find her and he'd never let her go again, no matter what.

That's what she'd said to him. *Believe in me, no matter what.* He clung to that now and held tight to the hope of finding her alive.

SEVENTEEN

Erin's pulse quickened as the driver turned the dark vehicle onto the winding paved road up to the Jeffries estate. Thunder boomed over the hillside and gray clouds made the wee hours of the night seem desolate and dismal. Dark memories swirled around her like black lace, tickling at her consciousness with hisses and taunts.

Her words to herself. *You let him die.*

Congressman Jeffries, talking to her in that patronizing, controlled tone the night he'd killed his son. *"I can't let you live, Erin. I'll have to make it look like you did this. It's the only way."*

Her voice screaming into the night. *"Please, please, let me call someone. Let me help him. He's going to die."*

He did die. He died right in your arms.

You could have saved Michael.

You should have run away before it was too late.

The congressman shouting orders to Leon Ridge. *"Shoot me in the arm, so it'll look as if she did it. Then get her out of here. And take care of her. Permanently."*

She'd relived the angry words and her own guilt over and over for the past six months. Michael's dying gaze had stayed with her. And even now as she dreaded being back in this place, she remembered details she'd tried hard to forget.

He'd tried to say something.

Erin could see it clearly now. Michael's bloody hand gripped her jacket. His frantic gaze moved from her to the table.

"Juan."

He'd called out Juan's name. That forgotten memory shouted out at her with each twist of the road. She'd connected on it briefly the night Chase mentioned Juan Gomez to her, but now she *was* positive Michael had been trying to tell her about Juan.

He'd said "Juan," and then his frantic gaze had shifted to the table. "There."

Erin closed her eyes and tried to remember the patio table.

Papers! She'd seen a set of papers lying on the table.

Had Michael been trying to tell her about the papers?

She turned toward Harland Jeffries, but the house loomed ahead of them, caught against the gloomy sky like a massive mausoleum. Could she do this? Could she go back to the place that had brought so many nightmares into her life?

She had to, for Michael's sake if nothing else. Michael deserved to have the people responsible for this brought to justice. He wouldn't have balked. Michael always found the truth. She had to do the same.

"We had such good times here, didn't we?" Congressman Jeffries reached for her hand and held it, the damp sweat from his palm causing her to shudder.

She couldn't speak. She tried to form the thoughts bottlenecking in her head in a crashing pileup. She could be wrong about all of it. The gun might be lost forever, thrown deep into the woods, or floating in a river somewhere. The papers could have been a bill the congressman was studying or some sort of contract he was working on.

"We're here," Jeffries said, his hand still caught in hers. He lifted a rifle up from the floorboard and strapped it over his shoulder. Then he pulled a hand-gun out from under his raincoat.

Erin closed her eyes and tried to draw another breath. All these months and now she was back here. She'd tried so hard to be strong, to build a case against Harland Jeffries so that she could prove her innocence. Would it finally end here tonight?

"You can't hide from me anymore, Erin. I brought you here because I thought this would be a fitting end for both of us."

"Not if Chase shows up." She turned to face the man who'd tormented her for so long. "The entire Capitol K-9 team will be looking for me."

"They won't find you in time, my dear. I've waited for this moment too long. By the time they arrive, you'll be dead. And I'll be gone. Gone away from everything I love."

Erin shivered, her body numb with a cold that wouldn't go away. How could she do this? She didn't want to die at this gloomy, sad place. She wanted to live and to love again.

She wanted to be with Chase again.

Then she thought of her beautiful, strong mother. Mom would want her to fight to the finish, to show courage in the face of tremendous odds. The only way she could come out of this whole was to face what she was afraid of most. And that wasn't Harland Jeffries or dying. Her worst fear stemmed from loving too much. She'd lost her mother. She'd lost Michael. What if she lost Chase?

She had to face that fear by staying alive to be with him.

God was with her. She had to believe that. Christ would give her strength.

So she took a deep breath.

It wasn't about the gun.

It was about those papers she'd briefly glimpsed on that table. And it was about finally facing her own horrible nightmares so she could bring Harland Jeffries to justice at last.

While the captain and several others walked with Leon Ridge as he tried to go back over his actions on that night, Chase and Valor combed the woods near the old barn over and over. The van they'd found was abandoned. Not a trace of anything, not even a clue from Erin.

What did he do now?

Chase mulled that over, but he wanted to get in there and get her out of this place. Things could turn ugly, even with a team hiding in the nearby woods around the vast property.

He checked in with the captain.

"We have to go in now," he said. "The less time we spend here, the better. If he doesn't have her inside that house, we have to start over."

Valor sat still with his ears lifted high as if he agreed with Chase's thoughts. They both needed to find Erin.

Lightning sizzled in a jagged line across the sky,

followed by a boom of thunder that made Valor give him another glance. Full darkness settled around them, the air hot with a cloying dampness. Another round of storms would hit soon enough. Chase didn't intend to linger.

Captain McCord gave him the go-ahead to get closer in on the house. "Take Adam Donovan with you and we'll be nearby with Ridge. Do not go in without backup, you hear?"

"Yes, sir." Chase radioed Adam and soon they were stalking toward the back side of the large sloping yard around the Jeffries house.

Erin followed Jeffries into the house, her breath coming in fast, shallow gulps. The smell of lemon wax and sweet potpourri hit her nostrils, reminding her of how much time she'd spent here over the past few years.

To the right past the kitchen, the big comfortable den brought back memories of watching football games and movies, sometimes with Michael and his father and other friends. Sometimes alone with Michael.

She could almost hear Michael's laughter, could see him jump up when his team made a touchdown. Watch him throw popcorn when his team lost. Michael didn't like to lose.

But right now, she remembered his father's anger and the wild look in the congressman's eyes as he glared at her and his dying son, a few feet away from him on the big patio by the pool.

"Why did you bring me back here?" she asked, her voice echoing out over the silent house like a wail.

He clutched her arm, his hand as rigid and hard as a talon, the smell of his wet, sweaty clothes assaulting her.

"Simple, my dear. You're my insurance policy while I search for something important. I decided if I can't get away then I will die here in the place I love. The place where my son died."

"Where have you been hiding?" If she could keep him talking, maybe he'd confess all to her. If she died with him, she'd at least die knowing the truth.

"Here and there, just like you," he retorted. "I just prefer hotels and country homes to running through the woods." He laughed and lifted his free hand in the air. "I've been back here several times. The matter of the gun—my gun—that Leon seemed to have misplaced forced me to take drastic, risky measures. Smart of him to confess so he could stay protected behind the jailhouse walls."

"But you sent lawyers to help him."

"I sent lawyers to delay him and to convince him to shut up. But that didn't work either. He has betrayed me. If I send anyone else, it will be to kill him."

Erin shuddered at that cold statement. So Leon had been willing to sit in prison rather than be out where this monster could find him. She couldn't blame him for that.

"And what about your other son?" she asked, wanting Jeffries to confess about Juan, too.

Harland Jeffries turned to stare down at her, his fingers digging into the sleeve of her hoodie. "I only had one son. Now shut up and move."

She shuffled in slow motion, but refused to look up the long hallway at the closed doors to the congressman's office.

He pushed her forward. "Toward the back and to the

left. There's a stairway down to the basement that's hidden from sight."

Erin didn't ask why he was taking her to the basement. She knew this house just about as well as he did. Michael had shown her the hidden passages. One of them had led the authorities to the congressman's safe room, where they'd found strong evidence of his corruption. But there were other hidden closets and small rooms underneath this massive structure.

If only she could find something to prove the rest of his crimes. Or some way to make him confess so someone would know about it before it was too late.

They moved across the dark planked floors, each creak of the aged wood like a warning. The congressman's bodyguard touched a gloved hand to his phone flashlight, causing the shadows to scurry away.

"Leave us," the congressman told the big man. "I know my way around my own home. You need to guard the entryway."

The guard turned and walked back toward the front of the house.

"Everything looks the same," she said. "This house was always immaculate. You demanded that."

"Yes," he said in a conversational tone that indicated they might be going in to dinner. "I demanded the best from my staff, my constituents and my family. Michael disappointed me. Leon is a coward and Rosa only used me for her own gain. You let me down, too." He shook his head. "It's all such a shame, isn't it?"

"Yes," she retorted. "A terrible shame."

But she wasn't referring to the people he'd mentioned.

It was a shame that a powerful man had turned into

a horrible, evil creature she didn't even know. It was a shame that Michael had to die because of this man's corruption and lies, and that she'd had to go into hiding for months now.

She thought of Rosa as they moved through the kitchen. Poor Rosa, seduced by a man who'd had her killed in order to keep that power. Who'd killed his own son in order to keep the kind of power that made him think he was some sort of god.

Erin knew whom she could count on. But she also knew her time was running out.

You're his next victim.

Chase and Adam moved through the rain-soaked trees, their partners sniffing the ground and the air. When they reached a spot near the driveway, Chase heard footfalls moving away.

Valor alerted, his hackles rising. Adam's Doberman, Ace, growled low.

"Let me check it out."

Chase moved in front of Adam. He did a zigzag search through the trees, following Valor, his high-powered rifle at the ready.

"They must have brought her here in a car," he said when Adam returned without finding anyone. "But they must have hidden that vehicle. I think we alerted a foot guard."

Adam stilled Ace. "What now?"

"I need to get closer in," Chase whispered. "If Valor can pick up her scent, then we'll know she's somewhere inside that house."

"You go and I'll cover you," Adam said.

Chase nodded and moved through the tall shrubbery near the winding drive. "We've got to find Erin, boy."

Valor's ears perked up at the mention of her name.

Chase knew that feeling. His heart did the same thing.

When he heard a quick grunt and a thud behind him, he almost turned back, but Adam's voice in his ear alerted him to keep going. "One down," Adam said, his tone filled with victory. "Unconscious and cuffed to a tree."

Chase replied his acknowledgment and went on toward the looming mansion. When he reached the lush camellia bushes near the long columned porch, Valor alerted with a low growl.

Erin had to be in the house. But how was he going to get inside to find her?

She could hear her pulse in her ears, beating in a frenzied rhythm that had her dizzy with dread. Sweat beaded above her upper lip and moved like a sticky web down her backbone. She tried to inhale, but the cloying smell of the peach potpourri almost made her gag. She waited while the congressman opened the basement door.

"They took everything," he said in that same low, monotone voice. "All my important documents, my weapons, my laptops and anything they could find to implicate me for crimes I did not commit."

"I think you have that wrong," Erin said as he shoved her down the dark steps. "They have the proof they need to put you away for a very long time."

He tugged on a light, but it only flooded the big square room with a shadowy yellow gleam that showed off the cluttered shelves and creepy old furniture. The smell of something dank and musky replaced the scent of peaches from upstairs.

"They won't take me alive," he said. "I had to come back here one last time. Leon thinks he's so smart, playing games with me. But I'll make sure I take care of him tonight. And you'll be gone by then, too, dear Erin. Either with me or maybe even shot dead. A pity, but…you've caused me no small amount of inconvenience and aggravation."

"Inconvenience?" she shouted. "That's what you call me running for my life after I witnessed you killing Michael?"

He struck her, hitting her against her right cheek. She gasped and held a hand to her face. Warm, sticky blood colored her fingers.

"Shut up," he said on an angry growl.

Erin lifted her chin. "You won't get away with this."

"I've gotten away with much more," he retorted, the gun pressing against her ribs again.

Erin refused to panic. Chase would find her. She had to remember that. If anything happened—

She could feel the evil. She closed her eyes and wished she could blink them open and find herself safe with Chase, far away from here, and then she opened her eyes and decided she had to find a way out.

Congressman Jeffries had dismissed the one guard he'd allowed in with them, so she was alone with him. Now he grabbed her and shoved her toward a cabinet on a long wall of the basement, and then he hit a button on the wall. The cabinet moved to the left and a panel in the wall slid open to reveal a long narrow room lined with lighted glass cabinets. Empty glass cabinets.

The gun room. Erin had been down here once with Michael. He'd shown her some of the impressive weapons his father had collected over the years. One of those weapons had killed Michael. But that gun had probably never made it back to this room. She checked every shelf. Empty. Every drawer stood open and empty. Then she glanced behind her and saw the panel blinking near the door.

A security panel. These types of panels were all over the house. And…once when she'd been down here with Michael, he'd used the intercom to check with someone upstairs.

The intercom. Second button from the left? But she'd have to hold it down to speak into it. Or scream into it.

If she could activate the alarm system, that would at least make some noise. Would anyone hear?

Erin moved around the room, her mind whirling on how to find a way out. "I can't believe they'd take the weapons. They must have been looking for your gun." She glanced past the congressman and inched closer to the door. "Didn't you keep it in that fancy monogrammed box, the one back there on the last shelf?"

He pivoted and walked across the small space, giving her enough time to shift toward the partially closed door. She could take off upstairs or she could hit that button and hope someone would hear the alarm.

She was a foot away from the door when she felt his breath on her neck and the gun near her flesh. "Going somewhere, Erin?"

She turned to stare up at him, her right hand behind her, reaching, touching. "No. Okay, I thought about running, but…I'd never make it." She pretended to give in.

"I'm afraid, Congressman. I don't want to die. What do you want from me? Why are we back here?"

Tears formed in his eyes, but he didn't try to drag her back to the other side of the room. "I want my son back, but we can't make that happen, can we?"

Erin backed up an inch and slid two fingers against the computer system that ran the whole house. Then she halted.

She needed to know the truth. Now. Before she died. "Why did you have to shoot Michael?"

Congressman Jeffries frowned, his eyes growing misty again. "I didn't mean to. He just made me so angry. Michael always had an exaggerated sense of justice, just like his mother. Had to prove everyone wrong, including me. He…kept harping at me about…Juan and Rosa. I paid her, you know. I paid her extra to help with expenses. But Rosa wanted more. I gave her gifts to keep her happy, but she expected me to care about *him*. She threatened to expose me, ruin me. Her demands became so unreasonable."

"He was your son," Erin said, moving around so she could see the security panel. "He needed a father."

"I couldn't claim that child," Jeffries said, each word cluttered with agitation. "She knew that. She agreed to that. But Michael brought papers for me to sign. He'd found out the truth and he wanted me to set up a trust fund for that…that annoying little boy."

Papers. Was that why he was back here?

"Where are those papers now?" she asked, hoping he'd forget everything but that. Hoping she could whirl and hit a button, any button on that panel, and then she'd run for her life. Again.

"I don't know," he said in a candid admission. "I

thought maybe you might know, though. You need to tell me what you remember, Erin. Since my attempts to shut you up have failed, I decided to take matters into my own hands. I need those papers, and so here we are. I know you hid them somewhere. Did you and Leon conspire against me?"

"What are you talking about?" she shouted. "Why would I hide anything here in this horrible place?"

"Because you were always out to do me in," he said, his breath hissing like an electrical wire.

"I never did anything to you," she retorted, anger brimming over. "And I don't know what happened to those documents. Maybe Leon had someone take them."

"No, you're lying. You need to tell me what you did with the papers. You must have seen them lying there on the table that night."

"What does it matter now?" she asked, amazed at his lack of logic and reasoning. "Michael is dead and Leon is in custody. I only saw the papers once, on the patio table, and I've been running since then, so how could I have possibly hidden them? You've brought me back here for nothing, Congressman. They'll find me and then you'll have nothing left. Nothing."

He lunged toward her but stopped short. "Oh, but I have one thing everyone wants, my dear. You."

Erin kept talking, trying to stall him. "I'm not the one you want. You miss Michael, don't you?"

"He made me sign the papers," Jeffries shouted at her. "Told me he'd expose me himself if I didn't do it." He sighed, wiped at his eyes. "That brat stands to receive most of my fortune. Especially now that…my real son is dead."

So that explained it. Erin gulped a breath, wishing

someone else could have heard this confession. "You killed Michael and forced me to run because you don't want Juan to have any of your money?" She shook her head and once again inched toward the control panel. "Rosa is dead. Michael is dead. Your staff is gone and your reputation is already ruined beyond repair. Leon is out there right now, searching for the gun and any bullet fragments that can prove he tried to kill me on your orders, and yet you've brought me here on a fool's mission because you're still worried about your money?"

Jeffries stomped toward her. "I won't let that little boy ruin what's left of my hard-earned fortune." He leaned close. "Leon isn't talking about that, but his silence won't save him. I know they have him out in the woods right now, trying to find the gun, but he'll be dead before he reaches that spot."

He grabbed Erin and shoved her back against the big steel door, causing her hip to hit hard. She winced at the pain and regained her footing before she turned to face him. "And what about me? You'll kill me just to prove a point? You think I have those papers? If I did, I would have turned them over to the authorities by now. It's over, Congressman. You've run out of options."

His chuckle sent a chill down her spine. "You'll be dead by the time they find me. Unless they let me take you with me, of course. Just until I get away from here. But if you tell me where those papers are hidden, I might be able to let you live."

She knew that was a lie. He'd make sure she never talked to anyone again.

"I don't know where the papers are," she said. "I remember seeing papers on the table, but—"

"Leon let it slip that you probably knew where the papers were hidden since they were lying there that night. He implied you'd hidden them here so someone would find them, so I'd be implicated in Michael's...accident."

Leon. Trying to save his hide. "Leon is lying to all of us," she retorted. "I haven't been back here since that night."

"How can I believe you?" he asked, stalking toward her. "You'll die if you don't help me."

"Not if I can stop you," she shouted. Then she whirled and hit the buttons on the security panel. When nothing happened, her heart sank and Erin took her last hopeful breath.

But then a green light danced across the console, silently announcing someone had entered the front door.

Her gaze crashed with Harland Jeffries's and he grabbed her and held her in front of him. "I think you're lying," he said on a slithering breath. "But it's too late for you now, Erin. It won't matter if you hide those papers here or anywhere else. You won't live to show them to anyone."

Chase made it to the front porch and tried the door. Then he reported back to Adam. "Door's open. I'm headed inside," he said. "Stand watch while I check around."

"Got it," Adam replied. "No sign of any more hostiles."

Chase slipped inside with Valor, his heart skipping a couple of beats. Darkness shrouded the mansion. Valor bristled and stood tall, his ears up, his nose in the air.

"Is she here, boy?" Chase whispered, praying they could find her in time. He hurried up the long, wide hallway, checking doors and rooms, all the while talk-

ing to Adam through the radio. Where had Jeffries
taken her?

Adam reported back. "Chase, they found the gun
hidden inside the barn floor and the crime-scene techs
found the slug. It was near where Erin said, embedded in one of the barn planks. Looks like it's a match,
but the techs will do a comparison in the lab. Ridge
is sweating, though. He knows his freedom has gone
down the drain."

"Roger that," Chase whispered. "Now we have to
find Erin."

"I'm right behind you," Adam replied. "We all are.
Found one guard hiding out in the garage."

Chase acknowledged that and kept searching. The
team had always been behind him, even when he'd
doubted everyone.

He went in, knowing he could count on the captain
and everyone else to help him tonight.

When he didn't find anyone in the downstairs room,
he started upstairs. But Valor tugged toward the back
of the house.

And then, Chase heard a sound. A step against wood.
A drawn-out echo of a door slowly opening. Maybe
below?

The basement?

Waiting behind a door near the stairs, Chase silenced
Valor and held his breath. When he heard footsteps hitting against boards, he checked his weapon and waited.

But he didn't have to wait long.

"Officer Zachary, I'm here with dear, sweet Erin.
Won't you join us?"

Valor alerted and sent out a low growl. Somehow,
Jeffries had heard them approaching.

Chase stared through the faint light and saw a shadowy figure standing near a wall toward the back of the house.

"Erin?" he called out. "Are you all right?"

"I'm here," she said. "I'm okay, but—"

"Shut up," the congressman said, advancing toward Chase. "I have a gun on her," he called to Chase. "I'll shoot her if you make one wrong move."

Lightning lanced like a spear through the sky, giving Chase a visual. Valor growled and started barking. Chase couldn't shoot. He might hit Erin. And he couldn't release Valor. The congressman was using her as a shield.

"Let her go," Chase said, while the thunder and lightning clashed and opened a deluge of rain outside.

"Not just yet. I need something, and maybe my former aide Leon can help us since our dear Erin refuses to cooperate."

"What's that?" Chase asked, a hot wind moving over him from the open door. He switched on his radio and prayed the others would hear.

"A contract my son forced me to sign. Leon implied dear Erin had hidden those papers here to implicate me. Why don't you ask him about that? And soon."

"I'll see what I can do," Chase replied, sweat beading on his upper lip. "I need to radio to Ridge, okay?"

"Make sure that's all you radio. I'll kill her if one more person walks through that door. You know I will."

Chase believed the man. "Erin, hang on," he said.

"Just do it," the congressman shouted. "Before I lose my patience entirely."

The house went dark again, but one brief clash of

lightning lit the sky long enough for Chase to advance a step or two. The hallway was empty now.

Chase made the call to Captain McCord. "He has Erin and he thinks she knows about some papers she saw that night. Ridge told him Erin might have hidden the papers here as proof against the congressman's claims. A contract that Michael had him sign. Proof, sir. Final proof. He brought her here to find the contract. He wants to talk to Ridge, or he'll kill Erin."

"We've moving in dark," the captain replied. "I'll talk to Ridge."

"Roger that." Chase ended the call and whirled back toward the kitchen. But Jeffries was now standing in front of the office, Erin in front of him.

"Call off your dedicated team," he shouted. "I've decided since you alerted too many people, I just need to get out of here. With Erin. You've ruined my plans, but I always have a plan B."

"Not this time," Chase called. He slowly leaned his rifle against the wall and brought out his handgun. "Leon Ridge showed my captain where he hid the murder weapon. And we found the slug that will match up to your gun. With Leon's testimony and Erin's, too, we'll send you away for a couple of lifetimes at least." He inched up the hall. "You will never make it out of here, Congressman."

"I said I'm leaving," the congressman called. "And I meant it."

He'd moved from room to room, zigzagging through the connected rooms and making it hard for Chase to get a bead on him. But each time Chase saw Jeffries, the man had Erin in a vise grip he used like a shield.

Chase held his gun trained on the shadowy figure.

Valor lifted his head, a low growl emitting from between his bared teeth. "Don't make me shoot you, Jeffries."

"How about I just shoot you instead," the congressman called. Then he lifted the gun he held.

Chase heard a whish of sound and then fell to the floor, his gun clattering loudly as it hit the marble hallway. Stunned and writhing in pain, Chase searched for his weapon, his hand touching the hardwood floor. Valor started barking, but he went down in a whimper. He tried to get up but whimpered again and collapsed in a lump near Chase.

Then the man who'd disabled both of them came toward Chase like a figure out of a horror show and kicked Chase's gun across the hall, out of reach.

Erin screamed, but Jeffries now had an assault rifle aimed at Chase. "Shut up or I will blow him and that dog away."

Chase moaned and reached out a hand.

Erin's stomach roiled with all the force of the raging thunder in the heavens.

"What have you done?" she asked Jeffries, knowing everything he'd done. She realized the gun he'd held on her had been a Taser weapon. She could have gotten away, but it was too late now.

He grabbed her and shoved her back toward the basement stairs.

Erin screamed and struggled to turn around and take one last look at Chase. He tried to stand, but fell back to the floor, his hand reaching out toward her before the congressman shoved her around the dark corner and down the basement stairs.

"Erin?" Chase's weak call moved up the hallway.

"Chase, I'll be okay. I promise. I'll find a way."

"You should have kept running," Harland Jeffries whispered in her ear. With a cruel twist on her arm, he pushed her ahead of him, the steel of a gun pressing into her ribs.

"Chase," she said through a sob. "Chase…I'm so sorry."

"As well you should be," Jeffries said. "Now get down these stairs."

The congressman shoved her into the gloomy basement and slammed the door shut behind them and latched it, and Erin accepted that she might not ever see Chase again.

EIGHTEEN

Chase lay immobile for a few minutes, the effects of the Taser's electroshock slowly wearing away. Erin! He had to find Erin.

Hitting his radio, he called into the speaker, "Get in here! He's taken Erin."

He crawled toward the spot where the congressman had shoved his gun. Then he managed to stand, the vertigo making the room spin. Grabbing a door facing him, Chase lifted himself up and searched the dark hallway. Then he saw Valor.

"Up," he called, his voice weak. "Valor, go."

The dog whimpered and lifted his head. Had the congressman drugged him with a tranquilizer gun? Or had he used the Taser weapon on the canine?

When Chase heard boots hitting the porch, he headed to the front, but the door crashed open. Then the house filled with officers and canines.

Adam Donovan rushed to Chase. "Which way?"

"Basement," he said, pointing. "I'm fine. Go. Go!"

Adam and his K-9 partner, a Doberman named Ace, stomped off toward the back. McCord and several others broke apart, left and right, to sweep the first-floor level of the house.

"Valor's down," Chase said. "Either stunned or doped. What took so long?"

"We had some setbacks," John Forrester shouted. "Dogs got restless, so we did a search in the woods."

"He must have planted some kind of scent to mess with them," Adam Donovan added as he hurried back to them. "But we did find a couple more guards scrambling to get away."

"We'll take care of him, Chase," someone shouted. Isaac Black.

It looked as though the entire team had been in on this. Chase was grateful for that.

"I lost her, Captain," Chase said. "But I'm going after her."

"Whoa." McCord tried to hold his shoulder, but Chase wasn't about to sit this one out.

"He brought her in here, sir. I'm getting her out."

McCord studied him for a minute and then nodded. "Get your head straight and go. We'll spread out and catch up with you after we finish searching the house."

Chase hurried to check on Valor. But the big dog lifted his head, stood up and barked as if to say, "I'm okay." Then he sat back and finally curled onto the floor, his head still up.

"Stun gun," Adam called while he moved around. "We found it near Valor. He's up but not quite ready to go."

All of this happened in a matter of minutes, but to Chase it felt like hours. He checked his weapon and started updating while he hurried toward the basement.

"I think he took her down there to an exit door."

McCord followed. "We have Ridge in the patrol car."

"He decided not to wait to talk to Ridge," Chase said. "The man's deranged. He thinks Erin knows something about a contract he signed, and that she purposely planted it here for us to find."

McCord nodded. "Ridge knows all about it. He threw Erin under the bus on that one, hoping the congressman would bring her here and kill her. But he's singing now. Afraid we'd hand him over to Jeffries."

"Where are the papers?" Chase asked as they fanned out through the empty basement.

"Ridge had his helper take them that night. They're in a safe-deposit box at a local bank. We're sending someone to verify that right now."

Chase didn't bother answering. He was on his way to the basement door when his cell buzzed. His heart thumped a warning.

"Zachary."

"You need to listen to me, Officer Zachary."

Chase held up his hand to halt the others. "I'm listening."

"Good. I'm used to people doing my bidding, so you're wise to follow suit."

"If you hurt her—"

"Now, now. That's not listening. Threats won't work with me. As you can see, I always get my way. I decided I do want those papers."

Chase closed his eyes and took a calming breath, the rage burning through him giving him enough adrenaline to clear his mind. "We have someone retrieving the papers now. Let her go."

"I can't do that until I see those papers with my own eyes. I want to walk out of here with just a couple of things. My papers and…Miss Eagleton." A long sigh. "I have your precious girl. But I need you to bring me my documents. Or you won't ever see her alive again."

Chase drew a hand to his forehead to steady himself. "Just give me Erin and I'll make sure the papers are destroyed."

"It's not that simple," Jeffries stated. "There are consequences and someone has to pay for that, too."

"Yes, well, how about *you* need to pay for that?"

McCord came up to Chase and shot him a warning glare. "Do I need to talk to him?"

Jeffries must have heard. "Tell Captain McCord I'm done with him. He let me down."

"I'll pass that on to the captain." Chase shook his head at McCord and tried to regroup. "Why do you need to take Erin out of here? We've put together a pretty good timeline on what happened that night. She didn't do anything wrong. She had to run for her life since Leon Ridge wanted her dead, too."

"Pretty good explanation, but not good enough to save my reputation," Jeffries shouted. "I'm ruined." Chase heard a shuffling noise and then he heard a small scream. "Ruined because Erin Eagleton had to show up unwanted. She ruined me. You all ruined me."

"Where are you taking her?"

"Why don't I let dear Erin tell you that?"

Chase waited, praying. "Erin?"

"I'm here," she said, her voice shaky. "I'll be okay. I know the truth now. Just get Leon out of there so he can tell the real story. We're in the woods—"

"She will not live!" Chase heard more shuffling. "If you don't get me what I need, I'll shoot her right now."

Chase mouthed *woods* to McCord. Then he grabbed the captain's sleeve and mouthed, *Check on Ridge.*

McCord went into action, motioning for the others to fan out and do another search. Then he motioned for Chase to buy more time while he got on his phone.

"Where are you planning to go?"

"Why are you wasting my time asking questions?" Jeffries shouted. "You can't stall the inevitable. Leon Ridge defied me and now he will pay for his betrayal. Erin defied me and she will pay. Even my own son betrayed me. After all I've done for this country and my state and those kids. All those poor, disillusioned children at All Our Kids foster home. I helped all of them over the years. All of them. Including your heroic Captain McCord."

"Except one," Chase said. "Congressman, there's still time to work something out. You have another son, remember?"

"No. No. That boy will never be a true Jeffries. Nothing will ever be the same, and someone has to pay. I want you to call off those dogs and that SWAT team your commander has already alerted."

Chase swallowed the bile forming in his throat. "Okay, all right. I'll bring you the papers. Just...don't take Erin with you. She can't hurt you anymore and you don't need to hurt her any longer."

"Someone has to pay," the congressman said again.

The phone went dead.

Chase pocketed his phone and described the conversation. "He has her somewhere on this property and he wants us to exchange the contract for Erin. He must have taken her through the basement exit. He's gone from irrational to delusional. He knows it's over."

McCord kept barking orders. "It might not be logical to us, but we have to do as he wants until we can corner him." He started issuing commands about perimeters and coordinates, but Chase wasn't listening.

"Zachary, don't be stupid," the captain called. "Wait!"

"With all due respect, sir, I waited long enough."

Then he ran up the stairs and started toward the back of the house. When he heard a *woof*, Chase bolted back around to where an officer was sitting with Valor. Valor came trotting toward him.

"No, boy, stay," he commanded. Valor stood firm, his dark eyes full of a resolve and determination that almost broke Chase. This canine had the heart of a warrior and the strength to overcome any obstacles.

"Let's go find her," Chase said, deciding he could be the same. Jeffries wanted the last shred of evidence, but that didn't matter now. He was guilty. And it could be proved in court.

He and Valor took off out the door, the storm scurrying after them in a slash of lightning and thunder that danced across the heavens.

Erin gritted her teeth against the biting rain. They tromped through a trail deep inside the forest behind the Jeffries estate. She'd tried to leave clues, but with little on her, and with the congressman holding her in front of him, it wasn't easy. She had no sense of direction or time or hope.

She had only a prayer.

Please, help us, Lord. Help all of us.

She didn't try to speak or persuade him. Harland Jeffries was too far gone for that. He was a desperate, deposed dictator who was used to having his way. He'd only pretended to be a dedicated policy maker and politician.

"It's your fault," he said to her, his words hissing through the air. "Making me run like a common criminal." He shoved her forward, and Erin held on to her wet, drooping hoodie. "You should have minded your own business that night. I could have pinned this on Leon since he had already threatened me—about that Rosa woman."

Erin struggled to stay on her feet, her hands grasping for anything to hold her up. When her jacket fell forward, she noticed the weight of her notebook in her pocket.

And regained some of her hope.

If she could distract him, she could leave a trail.

"Why did Leon threaten you?"

Jeffries stumbled behind her just long enough for her to pull the soggy notebook out of her pocket. Hiding it against her stomach, she carefully flipped it open and started peeling off paper while she stomped and shifted to muffle the noise.

The rain aided her cause, so she kept talking. "I mean, you didn't care about Rosa. You didn't have anything to do with her death, right?"

He stopped and yanked her around. Erin barely had time to put one hand in her pocket. "You can't play games with me, Erin. You must know by now that this all started with that ungrateful woman. She wanted more money and when I wouldn't give it to her, she told me she'd just run off with Leon and that they'd tell the world the whole story."

Erin backed away, her hands in her pockets, shoved

together over her notebook. "So if I hadn't shown up that night, you would have called Leon to the estate anyway and he'd be the one being accused. But you tried to pin this on me."

She let out a chuckle. "Too late, Congressman. Leon's confessed to everything and he's implicated you, too."

He let out a low wail of frustration and then straightened and pushed her forward.

"Yes, well, Leon will regret his bad decisions soon enough." He moved in a small circle, his dark form a shadow in the gray-black of the forest. "Michael heard Rosa and me arguing, so he kept digging and pushing me until it was just too much. He knew it, all of it. And he threatened to go to the authorities. My own son."

Erin realized he was heading back toward the front of the property. Why?

She had to keep him talking. "Michael was trying to do the right thing after he found out that Juan was his half brother." She placed one hand over the other in her deep pocket, tearing away at pages.

The congressman shoved at her again. "The right thing? This is Washington, DC, Erin. Nobody ever does the right thing."

Erin thought she saw a light's beam behind them on the path they'd just traveled. "Some of us still believe in doing what's right, Congressman Jeffries. We try to do what's best for everyone, not just ourselves."

He slammed against her and almost knocked her down. "Shut up! I have one last thing to take care of before you and I wait on that infernal contract."

Holding Erin in front of him, he lifted the rifle strap off his shoulder and stared through the weapon's scope. Erin screamed and closed her eyes. She heard the swish of a silencer. When she opened her eyes, the man beside her had a soft smile on his face.

Jeffries stared through the scope. "Goodbye, Leon, my old friend. Go to your precious Rosa now."

Had he shot Leon?

When his cell buzzed, Erin saw her chance to either run or drop pieces of papers everywhere. The man couldn't conceive that he was finished. Done.

But she couldn't risk being shot in the back. Not when she knew Chase was so close.

She waited, praying that Chase wasn't far behind them. And while she waited, she took slow, measured movements to make sure someone would know they'd been on this muddy, rocky path.

Because if they didn't come soon, she was about to run for her life once again.

NINETEEN

"So the chopper is bringing the papers from the safe-deposit box Leon told us about. We'll retrieve the papers, and Jeffries will get on the chopper after he sees the papers. We get Erin out of there and then we take out Jeffries." McCord shouted over the wind. "Zachary, you get out there and make the exchange and get Erin, but…let him go. We'll take him down."

Chase listened and nodded, but he wanted to keep moving. He couldn't be sure Erin and Jeffries were on this path. The dogs had followed the trail in spite of the wind and the rain. Now the rain had settled to a light drizzle but the paths were muddy, slippery and nasty. Hard to pick up a trail.

Captain McCord had called in one more favor with General Meyer. The chopper would set down on Jeffries's private landing area so Chase could make the exchange. Jeffries's precious papers for Erin. McCord had called Jeffries to let him know they had what he wanted.

The snipers were already surrounding the area, with an order to shoot to kill if necessary. Jeffries had caused enough problems. He was a wanted criminal and he'd covered his crimes for far too long. He'd killed his mistress and his son, and he'd tried to kill Erin, too. He had nowhere to hide.

So now they were spreading out through the woods in a net that would capture a madman. And save the woman Chase loved.

McCord came running up to Chase. "More news, son. Leon Ridge is dead. Shot with a silenced high-powered rifle."

"I thought we were guarding him," Chase replied, fear for Erin ramping up.

"We were. Had guards surrounding the car. He leveled him with a single kill shot right to the head. Shattered the side window into the patrol car."

Chase listened to the captain and then headed out again on the same path, ahead of the pack. The wind and rain slashed at him with a razor-sharp assault, but he kept moving.

He and Valor stomped through the mud, the canine stopping here and there to do a ground search. When Valor alerted a few yards ahead of the others, Chase held his flashlight down so he could study the roots and muddy dirt.

The light hit on something in the mud. A few shoe indentions and something else. Chase squatted and ran his gloves over the wet dirt. Paper. Little torn pieces of paper tossed just off the muddy trail. He lifted one jagged, tattered slip. Black ink smeared across the curled edges. The handwriting caught his eye.

Pages from Erin's journal.

"Good job, Valor," he said, rewarding his partner with a quick pat and a hug. "Let's get going."

They kept at it, Chase shining the light and Valor

sniffing out more pieces of the journal. Erin was leaving them a trail that told more than just her location.

The journal that she'd carried with her all of these months held her thoughts and her fears, but now it might help to save her life. All the more incentive for Chase and Valor to find her and bring her home.

Erin heard a chopper off in the distance. Exhausted, wet and cold, she saw the first rays of dawn and what looked like a clear sky. Had they really been out here most of the night? It did seem like an eternity since Jeffries had taken her off the path and through streams and hills to hide their scent. Every now and then, she thought she heard footsteps behind them. But maybe that was just the echo of her prayers.

"Why don't you give yourself up?" she asked Jeffries. She'd tried to figure out a way to run, but with the darkness and his threats to shoot to kill, she decided to wait until the last possible moment.

And first light.

If she knew Chase, he'd have every law officer within a hundred-mile radius stalking through these woods to get to her before Jeffries could kill her. That would give her the chance she needed.

"I can't give up, so I need you as insurance, dear Erin," the congressman said as they moved down toward an open meadow. "I have to get away for good this time, with the only papers that can prove Juan is mine. Your Officer Zachary is bringing my documents to me in exchange for your life."

Chase would do that for her. She loved him so much.

Erin wondered why Jeffries hadn't just gotten rid of the gun and the contract that night instead of asking

Leon to wound him. "You trusted the wrong man to help you destroy the evidence," she said. "I guess you figured you could intimidate Leon into doing anything you wanted, but you were wrong."

Growing angry again, he grabbed her by the arm. "I trusted you, too, even when I told my son you didn't really love him."

"I obviously loved him more than you did," she retorted.

He slapped her and then dragged her down a cluster of rocks and saplings. Erin's arm burned in a twisted protest as her body hit against the jagged rocks and sharp twigs in a stabbing, grinding rag-doll descent. Gritting her teeth so she wouldn't cry out, Erin refused to show any more fear.

Then she saw the chopper blades swirling in the faint light of dawn. She had only a few minutes to make a run for it.

Chase and Valor topped the hill near the meadow as the sun's first piercing yellow rays crested the horizon to the east. He saw the chopper waiting on a level part of the big, open field. Searching the nearby wet woods, he rubbed at his eyes and repeated the silent prayer that had screamed through his thoughts for hours.

Help me to do my job to the best of my ability, Lord. Help me to save the woman I love.

Behind him in the dense woods, the entire Capitol K-9 team waited along with a SWAT team. McCord had warned Chase that Jeffries might force Erin up on that chopper and hold the pilot at gunpoint, but that was not going to happen.

When his cell buzzed, he ducked down to answer.

"Zachary, our shooters can't get a bead on Jeffries. He's making sure he has Erin too close for comfort."

"Roger that," Chase said. "Sir, please don't let anyone get trigger-happy. I have to get down there and pry Erin away. Valor will help with that, so I don't need anyone getting ahead of the game."

"Not a chance. We've worked too hard to keep this woman alive." Then a pause. "And…I owe you that much for doubting you."

Chase wasn't worried about doubts right now. "I think I can get to her. Valor loves Erin. He can take down the congressman and…she can run."

Erin had developed a knack for running, but Chase hoped to end that trend today. The next time she had to run, he wanted it to be straight into his arms.

"We'll provide backup on that," the captain said.

Chase closed his phone and waited. The timing had to be just right.

Erin cringed when she saw the black chopper waiting with whirling blades in the level center of the big meadow. Jeffries probably waited here for deer to cross the meadow during hunting season. She could almost imagine this angry, deranged man taking aim on a beautiful creature and bringing it down.

"It's time to move," he said, glancing around. "If your young man doesn't hurry, he'll find you dead and me gone."

"I thought you wanted the last of the evidence," she said, trying to stall him. "You have to meet Chase for the exchange. Your papers are on that helicopter, right? You'll be free soon. Don't you want that?"

"I do, but…it doesn't much matter now, does it?" He

gave her a glassy-eyed stare. "You just need to die, Erin. You can spend eternity with Michael, wherever he is."

Anger jarred Erin's adrenaline awake. Did this man think he could kill her in cold blood and then get away? Would he force her on to that helicopter?

He yanked her by her arm, sending a shattering pain throughout her shoulders and back. "Let's get this over with," he hissed in her ear, spittle at the corner of his mouth.

He shoved her out into the clearing and then brought his rifle up. Using her as a shield, he walked them toward the middle of the meadow. "Don't try to run. I'll maim you for life and make you wish I'd killed you."

Erin closed her eyes to that threat and thought about Chase and how he'd held her and comforted her, even on that first night when he'd found her. Even when he'd doubted her. Even when he hadn't quite forgiven her for leaving him behind.

She longed for that kind of unconditional love, and when the image of Christ came into her tired, scared mind, Erin found the last shreds of her strength. She did have that kind of love.

And if the worst happened, she'd take that love any day over the threats of a madman.

With that comforting thought front and center, she didn't struggle and she didn't try to run. Because she knew the truth and she believed with all of her heart that Chase would come for her.

"Hey!"

Chase called out over the row of the chopper, his heart swirling and twirling in a beat that moved much faster than those rotating blades.

Jeffries pivoted, Erin out in front of him, his wizened face hard with anger and the sheen of madness. Holding the rifle against Erin's back, he inclined his head.

Chase and Valor started across the meadow, Chase calculating how to grab Erin away so one of the snipers could bring down the congressman.

Jeffries saw Valor and shook his head. "Leave the dog behind, Zachary."

Chase stopped. "Stay," he commanded.

Valor looked confused, but the big dog stood still and then sat to wait, his eyes on Erin.

Chase was ten feet away from where Jeffries had pulled Erin underneath a mushrooming oak tree. Which made it hard for the snipers to get a good shot. The helicopter's blades caused the tree to shake and shimmy, but it was far enough away that they should be able to make the exchange.

"I'm here," Chase said, his gaze hitting on Erin. He pointed to the chopper. "Your papers are inside."

"I need proof," Jeffries said. "Let's walk to the helicopter, and you can show me."

Chase nodded. He'd do whatever it took to get Erin away from this deranged man.

Erin looked remarkably calm, considering she had an assault rifle pointed at her backbone—her eyes were as translucent and clear as the newborn sky. She gave him a quick, concise smile and then stood still by Jeffries.

"Did you bring the original contract?"

He nodded at Jeffries. "Yes"

They hurried to the helicopter, and Chase indicated to the officer inside to hand him the envelope.

Once that was done, Chase turned to Jeffries. "Here."

Jeffries shook his head. "Open it."

Chase moved closer, his every instinct telling him to run and grab Erin away from this monster. But he couldn't do that. Not yet.

When he got closer, the congressman pushed Erin forward. "Get the envelope, Erin. If you make one wrong move, I'll shoot both of you."

Erin nodded and gave Chase another quiet stare.

"Don't try anything," Jeffries called. "Give her the envelope and let her bring it to me."

Chase shook his head. "No. That wasn't part of the deal. I get her, and you get the envelope. Take it and get out of here."

"Do it my way, Officer," Jeffries called. "Or she will get a bullet to her back."

A static came through his earbud. "Can't get a good shot. Tree's blocking from this angle." Then another voice. "Repositioning."

Erin was a foot away. She reached out to take the envelope. "Just let me go, Chase. Let me go."

"Never." He handed her the package, their fingers brushing together like a whisper of a kiss. "Don't give up, Erin."

"Never," she repeated back to him.

And then she turned and shoved the envelope toward the congressman.

After that, the world shifted. The congressman pulled her with him toward the chopper. "We have to get away."

Chase called after them to stop. "Hand her over, Jeffries."

The congressman laughed and kept going. But the chopper pilot wasn't planning on giving him a ride. The blades whirled as the chopper lifted.

Chase was about to pull his own gun when he heard an angry growl, and then something fast and furry leaped into the air and ran toward the chopper.

Valor.

Chase pulled out his gun and shouted, "Jeffries, let her go."

The congressman forced Erin toward the helicopter, his gun now turned on Chase. Chase ran toward the chopper, ready to shoot to kill, but Jeffries fired a round of haphazard volleys that whizzed in the air and tore through the ground all around Chase.

Erin screamed and tugged, trying to get away. Chase ran behind Valor, desperate to help Erin.

But before he could get there, Valor hurled himself at the congressman and sank his teeth into the man's leg. Harland Jeffries screamed and writhed, falling on the ground in agony, his rifle firing up into the early-morning sky.

Chase screamed again. "Erin, get out of there." Waving his hands at her, he kept calling, "Erin?"

She scrabbled away and started toward him, but Jeffries reached out a hand and caught her leg. Valor sank his teeth in and tore at the man's thigh, dragging him until he had to let go of Erin. She took off, running toward Chase.

The chopper lifted away and circled back, and then landed again and sat with blades whirling. Then the field swarmed with law-enforcement people. Captain McCord made it to Jeffries first and commanded Valor to release, his rifle trained on the weeping, writhing man at his feet.

"It's over," the captain said as he hauled Jeffries up.

"You'll be serving in a different district from now on, but with a much longer term."

Chase saw Erin running toward him, Valor right by her side.

It was the most beautiful sight in the world.

He met her there in the dawn of a new morning and took her into his arms.

EPILOGUE

A crisp fall wind lifted out over the hills and valleys surrounding the brand-new barn Captain Gavin McCord had built on the ranch he'd purchased in Virginia. The captain had the barn to store equipment and hang out in, and a new house and a new facility nearby for the All Our Kids foster home. With General Meyer's help and funding from the Eagleton Foundation, not to mention donations coming in from all over the country, the new home would be renamed the Michael Jeffries Memorial Foster Home.

Chase sat with Erin inside the big open barn, his arm around her waist, his nose buried against her floral-scented hair. The whole team had been invited here to celebrate this new structure after they'd spent a lot of weekends helping the captain to build it.

But today was about much more than a new barn.

It was about a new beginning.

The barn was decorated with colorful fall flowers, and what Erin called garlands draped across the entryways and windows. Candles burned brightly in two tall glass holders, and the scent of new wood mixed with the sweet smells of the big cluster of bright orange, yellow and burgundy flowers centered at one end of the building.

Several rows of folding chairs parted in the middle to leave room for a center aisle. And soft music played by a quartet of fiddlers caused all of those waiting to stand and turn toward the back door.

Virginia Johnson came up the aisle first, carrying a simple bouquet of bright yellow flowers, her garnet-colored dress making her look less of a mousy woman and more of a stunner.

Chase smiled at Erin and saw approval and surprise in her pretty blue eyes.

The captain waited up by the makeshift altar with the local minister, looking more nervous than Chase had ever seen the man. And then a hush fell over the crowd gathered beneath the muted lights.

Cassie Danvers glided up the aisle in a lacy white dress that Erin had described as simple but elegant. Chase didn't know elegant from an elephant, but he had to agree Cassie looked nice.

He glanced from the smiling bride to the big man who'd stood by his side for six long months. Captain McCord looked happy. And in love.

"Can you believe this?" Erin whispered, her hand in his as they sat to watch Cassie and Gavin say their vows.

"Yes and no. I can't believe I'm sitting here with you."

She smiled and gave him a quick kiss. Then Chase listened to the sacred vows being said, his eyes on Erin. She teared up and tried to blink. But he couldn't resist reaching up to catch a single tear as it escaped down her cheek.

"I love you," he said.

"I love you back," she replied.

They'd said those words over and over, beginning with the day they'd watched Harland Jeffries being carted off in a paddy wagon. They'd held each other tight against the world, including the fellow officers who had to take their complete statements yet again and the relentless reporters who wanted to interview them or write books about them. They stood firm against Erin's father, when he'd finally sat them down at his house and surprised them by giving them his blessings.

And now, after seeing the captain and his bride so happy together, Chase knew he wanted the same with Erin.

After the ceremony was over, they all filed out of the barn to a pretty gazebo where a white wedding cake decorated with what Erin called "eatable mums" sat centered on a lace-covered table, waiting to be served up.

"Cake," Nicholas Cole said, pointing to the tiered concoction before he pointed to the other cake. "And K-9s." His fiancée, Selena Barrows, giggled. They were still planning their wedding, too.

They all laughed at the groom's cake, a chocolate sheet cake with miniature dogs placed across the top in what looked like a training yard. Big yellow letters stated Capitol K-9 to the Rescue.

"And barbecue," Isaac Black called out. "I'm starving."

"You're always starving," his bride-to-be, Daniella, said.

Everyone was here. Lana Gomez and Adam Donovan, who were going to be married in a month or so. Lana now had custody of little Juan. Veterinarian Jonas

Parker with Brooke Clark. They planned to marry and adopt more children to go with Jonas's son, Felix. And several others, including still-recovering Dylan Ralsey, his gunshot wound slowly healing, and serious but dedicated John Forrester.

Even Fiona Fargo, the redheaded whiz who'd worked lots of long hours to help them crack the Jeffries case.

Chase watched Fiona now—her bright blue eyes matched her peacock-embossed dress and high-heeled sneakers. When Chris Torrance walked up and winked at Fiona, Chase shot Erin a grin.

"I guess we can thank Fiona and Chris for giving all of us the love bug. I think they were the first couple to fall in love."

Everyone started clapping. "Like we didn't see that one coming," Dylan called out.

After everyone congratulated the captain and Cassie with cups of apple cider, Selena announced, "Hey, now that the captain is finally hitched, the rest of us can plan our weddings, right?"

"Right," Nicholas said with a shrug. "Out of respect for you, Captain McCord, we've all been holding off. But…it's on now, buddy. It is so on."

Chase laughed and clapped with the rest of them.

It *was* so on.

So he took Erin out onto the dance floor and while the fiddlers played a slow waltz, he danced with her and held her close. Then the music stopped and before he lost his nerve, he got on one knee and looked up at her.

Erin put a hand to her mouth. "Chase, what are you doing?"

He took in her shiny navy blue full-skirted dress and

the sapphire necklace she wore. "What do you think, beautiful? I want to ask you something."

She gasped and looked around while everyone laughed and smiled. "What?"

He pulled out a modest diamond solitaire ring. "Will you marry me, Erin?"

"Of course she will," Selena called out. "Tell him yes, Erin, already."

"Yes, yes." Erin smiled through her tears while he put the ring on her finger. Then he stood and kissed her.

"Double wedding," Selena shouted before she sailed into Nicholas's arms.

Soon everyone was hugging Erin and shaking Chase's hand.

Captain McCord came up and touched a hand on Chase's shoulder. "I'm happy for you, kid."

"Thank you, sir."

The captain didn't have to say anything else. They both knew how blessed they were.

Chase turned back to Erin, and together they took a stroll toward the autumn sunset gliding over a nearby valley.

"I miss Valor," she said. "He should hear our good news."

"He'll be at the wedding," Chase assured her. "He wants to be the best man."

"I think that's a perfect plan," Erin said. She tugged him close and kissed him. "It's nice to be running toward the sun, at last."

And then she took Chase with her as they did just that.

* * * * *

Dear Reader,

This was a tough story to write. We all get lost in the wilderness at times in much the same way as my heroine, Erin Eagleton, had become lost in the woods, running from fear and lies and injustice. But like Erin, we have to hold tight to our faith and look for the light that shines just outside the wilderness. Chase Zachary became Erin's light as he helped her to clear her name. They found a love that will hold them together during both good and bad times.

I hope you can find that kind of light through the love of Christ. He is there in the darkness with us, and He will carry us through destruction and guide us toward humility and honor.

I would like to thank the other wonderful writers who helped me so much while I was writing this book. Thank you to Shirlee, Terri, Lynette, Margaret and Valerie.

Until next time, may the angels watch over you. Always.

Lenora Worth

COMING NEXT MONTH FROM
Love Inspired® Suspense

Available September 1, 2015

THE PROTECTOR'S MISSION
Alaskan Search and Rescue • by Margaret Daley
As an Anchorage K-9 police unit sergeant, Jesse Hunt regularly puts his life at risk to rescue others. But he'll pull out all the stops when a bomber threatens his hometown—and his former high school sweetheart...

RODEO RESCUER
Wrangler's Corner • by Lynette Eason
Tonya Waters isn't about to fall for another cowboy bull rider, yet when handsome Seth Starke offers help escaping her recently freed stalker, she'll accept. She barely eluded the assailant before, and now he's after Tonya *and* Seth.

PLAIN THREATS • by Alison Stone
Ever since her husband's crimes left Rebecca Fisher an Amish widow, she's been targeted. To discover whether her stepson knows more than he lets on, Rebecca turns to his professor for answers. But the questions put them *both* in danger...

DESPERATE ESCAPE • by Lisa Harris
Former special ops agent Grant Reese is trained to defuse land mines—not rescue damsels in distress. But when Dr. Maddie Gilbert is kidnapped by drug traffickers, he'll face any threat to save the woman who's always held his heart.

EASY PREY • by Lisa Phillips
US marshal Jonah Rivers has never forgotten his brother's widow, Elise Tanner. When he finds her in a dire situation—with a nephew he didn't know existed—he'll stop at nothing until they're both out of harm's way.

EXPERT WITNESS • by Rachel Dylan
Tasked with protecting a sketch artist who is testifying in a high-profile murder trial, US marshal and former FBI agent Max Preston jumps into action to keep Sydney Berry safe. But can he save her from the secrets of her past?

LISCNM0815

REQUEST YOUR FREE BOOKS!
2 FREE RIVETING INSPIRATIONAL NOVELS PLUS 2 FREE MYSTERY GIFTS

RIVETING INSPIRATIONAL ROMANCE

YES! Please send me 2 FREE Love Inspired® Suspense novels and my 2 FREE mystery gifts (gifts are worth about $10). After receiving them, if I don't wish to receive any more books, I can return the shipping statement marked "cancel." If I don't cancel, I will receive 4 brand-new novels every month and be billed just $4.99 per book in the U.S. or $5.49 per book in Canada. That's a savings of at least 17% off the cover price. It's quite a bargain! Shipping and handling is just 50¢ per book in the U.S. and 75¢ per book in Canada.* I understand that accepting the 2 free books and gifts places me under no obligation to buy anything. I can always return a shipment and cancel at any time. Even if I never buy another book, the two free books and gifts are mine to keep forever.

123/323 IDN GH5Z

Name	(PLEASE PRINT)	
Address		Apt. #
City	State/Prov.	Zip/Postal Code

Signature (if under 18, a parent or guardian must sign)

Mail to the **Reader Service:**
IN U.S.A.: P.O. Box 1867, Buffalo, NY 14240-1867
IN CANADA: P.O. Box 609, Fort Erie, Ontario L2A 5X3

Are you a current subscriber to Love Inspired® Suspense books and want to receive the larger-print edition?
Call 1-800-873-8635 or visit www.ReaderService.com.

* Terms and prices subject to change without notice. Prices do not include applicable taxes. Sales tax applicable in N.Y. Canadian residents will be charged applicable taxes. Offer not valid in Quebec. This offer is limited to one order per household. Not valid for current subscribers to Love Inspired Suspense books. All orders subject to credit approval. Credit or debit balances in a customer's account(s) may be offset by any other outstanding balance owed by or to the customer. Please allow 4 to 6 weeks for delivery. Offer available while quantities last.

Your Privacy—The Reader Service is committed to protecting your privacy. Our Privacy Policy is available online at www.ReaderService.com or upon request from the Reader Service.
We make a portion of our mailing list available to reputable third parties that offer products we believe may interest you. If you prefer that we not exchange your name with third parties, or if you wish to clarify or modify your communication preferences, please visit us at www.ReaderService.com/consumerchoice or write to us at Reader Service Preference Service, P.O. Box 9062, Buffalo, NY 14240-9062. Include your complete name and address.

LIS15

Can K9 cop Jesse Hunt help Lydia McKenzie unlock her memories to catch a serial bomber?

Read on for a sneak preview of
THE PROTECTOR'S MISSION,
the next book in USA TODAY *bestselling author*
Margaret Daley*'s miniseries*
ALASKAN SEARCH AND RESCUE.

Lydia closed her eyes and tried to relax. But visions of the bombing assailed her mind. The sound of hideous laughter right before the bomb went off. The expression on Melinda's face when she knew what was going to happen. Was she alive? The feeling of helplessness she experienced trapped under the building debris. Her heartbeat began to race. A cold clamminess blanketed her.

Her hospital room door opened, pulling her away from the memories. When Lydia saw the person who entered, her pulse rate sped faster. Jesse Hunt. She wasn't prepared to see him.

He looked as if he'd come straight from the crime scene. As a search and rescue worker for Northern Frontier, he'd probably work as long as he could function. The only time he'd rest was when his K9 partner, Brutus, needed to.

So why is he here?

He stopped at the end of the bed. "Bree told me you were awake, so I took a chance and came to talk to you."

His stiff stance and white-knuckled hands on the railing betrayed his nervousness, but his tone told her he was here in his professional capacity. Saddened by that thought, Lydia said, "Thank you for finding me."

"I was doing my job yesterday."

"Knowing the people who would be searching kept my hope alive. Have you found everyone?"

"We don't know for sure. Names of missing people are still coming in. I was hoping you could tell me how many people were in the restaurant when the bomb exploded."

"I don't know…" The thought that the bistro was totally gone inundated her. She dropped her gaze to her lap, her hands quivering. Emotions crammed her throat. She turned for her water on the bedside table, but it was too far away. She started to lean forward and winced.

Jesse was at her side, grabbing the plastic cup and offering it to her.

She took it, and nearly splashed the water all over her with her shaking.

Jesse steadied the cup, then guided it to the bedside table. "I know this isn't easy, but anything you can remember could help us piece together what happened. We've got to stop this man."

"Nobody wants that more than me. I'm sure I'll remember more later." She hoped she could.

She needed to.

Don't miss
THE PROTECTOR'S MISSION
by Margaret Daley,
available September 2015 wherever
Love Inspired® Suspense books and ebooks are sold.